Richard Dowling

Tempest-driven

Vol. I

Richard Dowling

Tempest-driven
Vol. I

ISBN/EAN: 9783337066710

Printed in Europe, USA, Canada, Australia, Japan

Cover: Foto ©Andreas Hilbeck / pixelio.de

More available books at **www.hansebooks.com**

TEMPEST - DRIVEN.

TEMPEST-DRIVEN.

A Romance.

BY

RICHARD DOWLING,

AUTHOR OF "THE MYSTERY OF KILLARD," "THE WEIRD SISTERS,"
"THE SPORT OF FATE," "UNDER ST. PAUL'S," "THE DUKE'S SWEETHEART,"
"SWEET INISFAIL," "THE HIDDEN FLAME," ETC.

IN THREE VOLUMES.

VOL. I.

LONDON:
TINSLEY BROTHERS, 8, CATHERINE ST., STRAND.
1886.

CHARLES DICKENS AND EVANS,
CRYSTAL PALACE PRESS.

CONTENTS.

CHAPTER VI.

CHAPTER XIV.

CHAPTER XV.

CHAPTER XVI.

CHAPTER XVII.

TEMPEST-TOSSED.

CHAPTER I.

IN THE DEAD OF NIGHT.

It was pitch dark, and long past midnight. The last train from the City had just steamed out of Herne Hill railway station. The air was clear and crisp. Under foot the ground was dry and firm with February frost. All the shops in the neighbourhood had long since been shut. Few lights burned in the fronts of private houses. The Dulwich Road was deserted, and looked dreary and forlorn under its tall, skeleton, motionless, silent trees. There was not a sound abroad save the gradually-dying rumble of the train, and the footfalls and voices of the few people who had alighted from it. Little by little these sounds died away, and the stillness was as great as in the pulseless heart of a calm at sea.

Alfred Paulton had arrived by the last train. He was twenty-eight years of age, of middle height, and fair complexion. He lived in Half Moon Lane, and after saying good-night to some acquaintances who came out in the train with him, turned under the railway viaduct at Herne Hill, and walked in the direction of his home.

He was in no hurry, for he knew his father and mother and sisters had gone to bed long ago. He had his latch-key, and should let himself in. His ulster covered him comfortably from neck to heel. He had supped pleasantly with a few friends at his club, the Robin

Hood, and earlier in the day finished a very agreeable transaction with his solicitor, and now had in his pocket a handsome bundle of notes.

As he walked he swung his stick, and hummed in a whisper a few bars from the favourite air of a comic opera which he had been to hear that evening.

Suddenly he started. As he was directly opposite the door of a house, standing back a few yards from the road, the door opened noisily, and he heard a woman's voice in a tone of piteous entreaty exclaim:

"Oh, what shall I do — what shall I do?"

Alfred Paulton drew up and listened.

For a while all was silent.

He looked over the paling, which was just as high as his chin. In the doorway of the house stood the figure of a woman against the light of a lamp on a table in the hall. The leafless boughs of the intervening shrubs prevented his getting an uninterrupted view, but he could in a brief glance gather a good deal.

The figure was that of a woman neither tall nor short, neither stout nor thin. She was evidently not a servant. She wore an ordinary indoor costume, and had nothing on her head. Although she had scarcely moved since the opening of the door, he came to the conclusion she was of alert and active habit. He judged her to be neither old nor young. Her hair shone raven-black in the lamplight. The illumined cheek was finely modelled, dark in hue—that of a brunette. She leaned forward into the darkness, and peered right and left, moving her head but slightly as she did so. Something glittered in the starlight at her throat and at her girdle. Her hands were held behind her to balance the forward inclination of her body. On her fingers jewels sparkled in the lamplight of the hall behind her.

All this he saw at a glance. He was perplexed, and did not know how to act. It was scarcely fair in him to stand there eaves-dropping, as it were. If he moved now she would hear him, and know he had seen her and had stopped to listen. If he spoke he might alarm her.

Up to the moment the door opened and she appeared and called out, he believed this house to be empty. It had been vacant for a long time. Now he recollected having heard that it was let at last, and that the new tenant was expected to arrive this day. The place was called Crescent House. He had heard talk about the new-comers at the breakfast-table that morning; but nothing seemed known of them except that they came from a distance and were well off.

The woman in the doorway now straightened herself, raised both hands to her forehead, and moaned out in a lower and more despairing tone her former words :

" Oh, what shall I do—what shall I do ? "

He could hesitate no longer. It was plain she was in a sore strait. He coughed, advanced to the gate, and, putting his hand on the latch, said :

" I beg your pardon. Is there anything wrong ? "

She started back a pace into the hall. In doing so her full face met the lamplight for a moment. It was a very beautiful face, full of terror.

" Do not be alarmed," he said softly ; " I was passing when you opened the door, and I heard you speak. Is there anything wrong ? Anything I can do for you ? "

She seemed reassured, and stepped once

more to the threshold, and said, in a quick, low voice :

"I am a stranger here. I came to this house only to-day. I am alone with my husband in the house, and he has been seized by sudden illness. I do not know where to find a doctor, even if I could leave the house, and I cannot go away from my husband."

"In what way can I be of use ? Pray command me."

He tried to open the gate, but failed.

She perceived his efforts to open the gate, and once more withdrew a pace into the hall, crying in alarm :

"No, no; you must not come in ! If you wish to help me, go for the nearest doctor. Go at once. Do not stand there. In heaven's name, do not lose a moment ! Go, I implore you."

She clasped her hands, and held them out towards him in entreaty.

"As you wish," he said. "I shall not be many minutes."

He turned and ran back towards the railway station. Dr. Santley, the family physician of the Paultons, lived close by, and Alfred Paulton resolved to summon him, although he might not be exactly the nearest medical man. Time would be gained rather than lost by going for him, as Santley would come at once without waiting for explanations—that is, if he were at home.

On his way he had little space to think, the time being short and the pace quick. He was more lucky than he had hoped, for he almost ran over the man he sought at the gate of his house.

"Oh, doctor," he cried, almost breathless, "I am so glad to meet you up and dressed! I want you, if you will be good enough to come with me at once."

"Mr. Paulton, I'm sorry. What is the

matter? I have just come back from another unexpected patient."

"It's no one at our place, thank goodness! It's some one at Crescent House. I don't even know the name."

By this time both men were walking rapidly towards Half Moon Lane.

Dr. Santley was a tall, slender man, with full black beard and moustaches. He had a quiet, gentle, responsible manner, and rarely smiled. As the two strode on together, Alfred Paulton described the scene in which he had just taken part. When he had finished, his companion said:

"Ah, I saw the vans at the door to-day; but surely they cannot have got a big house like that straight in so short a time. Here we are."

They had arrived at the spot where a few minutes before the younger man had stood and spoken to the strange woman in the doorway. The door was now not open.

Paulton rattled noisily at the gate, and then waited a while. There was no answer. He looked at the windows of the house; none was lighted up. Light shone in the fan-sash over the door.

"You cannot have mistaken the house in the dark?" asked Dr. Santley, suppressing a yawn.

"Impossible! It was the only house to be let. It is Crescent House, and you yourself saw the furniture going in to-day."

Again he rattled the gate, this time as loudly as he could.

At length the door of the house was opened slowly, and against the light of the lamp the same figure as Paulton had seen before was revealed. Again the woman stood still on the threshold and leaned out into the darkness. This time she at once turned her face towards the gate.

Before either of the men had time to speak, she said in a calm, low, penetrating voice:

"Is the doctor there?"

"Yes," answered both in a breath.

"I will open the gate in a moment."

With a firm, swift step she left the doorway and trod the gravelled path leading to the gate. She did not hesitate or fumble at the latch. In a few seconds the gate swung open.

"This is Dr. Santley; he is our family physician. He and I live close by. May I offer you my card? I and my family will, I am sure, feel delighted to be of any service to you," said Paulton, raising his hat.

"Stay," she said. "Will you both come in? I am terrified. I do not know what has happened. I hope you are not too late."

Her words were measured and her tone calm. Although the trees overhead were leafless, where she stood was dark, and neither of the men could see her clearly.

Without further words she led the way

back to the house. The two men followed in silence. When they entered the hall she turned round in the full light of the lamp, and, stretching out her right arm towards the first door on the left, said :

"In that room. I shall wait for you. There is no other light. Take this lamp."

Paulton now saw her fully. She was dark, almost swarthy. There was no colour in her cheek. Her forehead was small and compact. Her eyebrows and hair jet, glossy. Her eyes were dark, large, a little sunken, brilliant, and full of suppressed fire. The nose was slightly aquiline. The only relief to the dark hue of the face and the black of the eyebrows, hair, and eyes, was afforded by the full, red, ripe lips. And all the features, the forehead, the nose, the chin, the mouth, the cheeks, were finely modelled. The face was commanding, imperial, triumphant. It was as set and firm as marble. It was the face of an empress born to lead her legions to victory—of a woman in whom courage was a matter of course, who regarded obedience to her wish as a spontaneous offering. She had the immortality of indestructible will in her face, the weight of irresistible determination.

With the face ended the heroic aspect of the woman.

At her throat blazed the diamonds of a brooch large as the palm of her hand. On her fingers glittered a dozen diamond rings. The belt round her waist was fastened with a diamond clasp. The diamonds at her throat held an orange-coloured silk scarf. The rest of her dress was dead black, close-fitting to the figure, and full of folds below the waist. The arms were bare half-way from the elbow to the wrist. The figure, the arms, the hands were subduingly soft and feminine. The arms and wrists were round, the hands exquisitely delicate, with fine taper fingers, the bust a miracle of rich symmetry.

It was the head of Boadicea on the figure of Rosamond.

Dr. Santley took up the lamp from the hall table and entered the room she had indicated. Paulton paused for a moment in doubt as to whether he should go or stay. The hall lay now in comparative darkness; there was no light except what came through the open door of the front room.

"Follow him."

It was her voice.

Paulton obeyed. As he got inside the doorposts he turned round and looked back into the hall. He could make out nothing but the glitter of the diamonds at her throat, in her girdle, on her fingers. They were stars against the darkness of her dress, as the stars abroad in heaven against the sightless robe of night.

The room in which Dr. Santley and Paulton found themselves was in the greatest disorder. In one corner lay the carpet rolled up, in another the hearth-rug, fender, fire-irons, and coal-scuttle. All along the right side stood a row of chairs, one inverted on another. Pictures rested on the floor with their faces against the wall; the gaselier sprawled close by the window; the leaves of the dining-table were set against the folding-doors at the back. The drawers and pillars of the sideboard were hard by, the top and back of it stretched upward into the gloom of a deep recess; several boxes and canvas packages littered the floor. Two knights in plate-armour reclined one at each corner of the chimney-piece; easy-chairs were wedged in among amorphous bundles wrapped in Indian matting; rods and poles protruded from under legs of chairs, under bales heaped upon one another.

A small table, face down upon another, held its slender legs up in air. Some fire still smouldered in the grate; the fire must have been large not long ago, for the room was still warm.

In the centre of the room stood the dining-table, reduced to its smallest dimensions. On this were spread the remains of a simple supper. Close by the table stood a couch, and on the couch appeared the figure of a man.

The figure was sitting up in the arm of the couch, the legs rested on the couch, the head drooped forward; the chin and lower part of the face were buried in the thick, long, grizzled beard that flowed down over the chest.

Dr. Santley stepped up to the couch on which the figure lay, and having placed the lamp upon the table close at hand, began his examination. It did not take long. After a few minutes he turned to Paulton, and, pointing to the figure, shook his head.

"Well?" asked the young man below his breath.

The doctor went up to him and whispered in his ear:

"Dead some time."

Paulton looked round apprehensively at the door, and whispered back:

"How will she take it?"

The doctor shook his head.

Both men stood staring at one another.

Suddenly both started; they heard a footfall behind them. Some one had entered the room.

CHAPTER II.

THE two men turned quickly round. The light of the lamp fell on the black dress of the woman and sparkled on her diamonds. Her arms hung down by her side. Both hands were clenched. She advanced with a steady, slow step, her eyes firmly fixed on Dr. Santley's face. She did not glance at Paulton. She did not glance at the couch.

"You were long," she said, in a slow, constrained voice, "and I came in to know."

She rested the tips of the fingers of

one hand on the table and kept her eyes
fixed on the doctor.

"I think," said Santley, placing himself
between her and the couch, "that it
would be better if we went into some
other room."

"We cannot; this must serve. All the
other rooms are locked up, except my
bed room, and my husband has the keys."

Her voice did not falter.

"Has Mr. ——, your husband, been long
ill?"

"My husband's name is Louis Davenport.
He has been ill a long time—years.
He has been suffering from spasmodic
asthma. I can gather from your manner
that there is no hope."

Her voice was firm and clear. No feature
moved but the beautiful, flexible mouth, of
which the lips were as full of colour as
ever.

"May I beg of you to be seated?" Dr.

Santley left the position he had occupied and handed her a chair. She sank on it without speaking. She rested one of her arms on the table. He went on: "Mrs. Davenport, I am afraid the worst must be faced."

"The worst!" she cried, rising and looking wildly at him, her voice now coming in a terrified whisper from between her lips, which at the moment lost their colour. "The worst! What do you mean by the worst? What do you know of the worst?"

Her face showed intense eagerness, mingled with intense fear.

"I am very sorry to be obliged to give you bad news."

"And it is?" with still greater eagerness and fear.

"That Mr. Davenport will not recover."

"That he is dead?" leaning forward on the back of her chair towards him.

"Unhappily, yes."

"Of his old disease?"

She still kept her eyes on Santley's face.

"Perhaps. Did he complain to-night?"

"Yes; he said he was too ill to think of lying down."

"He used, no doubt, to inhale chloroform when the spasms were bad?"

"Always."

"Yes, I got the smell of chloroform. Well, one of these spasms may have been too severe; and now you know the worst, Mrs. Davenport."

She sat down on her chair and seemed about to faint. There was wine on the table. Santley poured some into a glass and made her drink it. After a while she became composed, and the look of eagerness and dread disappeared wholly from her face, and the red returned to her lips.

She was the first to speak. Her voice had regained all its old, firm serenity. Her face was calm and commanding. She looked once more as though neither the onslaught of battle nor the wreck of worlds could disturb her.

"You, sir," she said, once more addressing Santley, "I have to thank for your promptness in coming at this hour to one whom you never even heard of before. And "—turning to Paulton—"I have to thank you most sincerely for your kindness in summoning the doctor for me in my extremity."

Each man protested he had in this matter done no more than his duty, and both said they sympathised with her in the awful calamity which had fallen upon her.

She bowed her head in acknowledgment of their kind-hearted speeches, and went on:

"I am, I may say, alone in the world

and without a friend in London. I am now, or shall be when you go, alone in this house. I do not know what is to be done in a case of this kind. For a long time I have been aware my husband might die at any moment. But now that this has happened, I find myself as unprepared for it as though the possibility of his death had never before entered my mind. I would therefore ask you to add to the favours you have already conferred by telling me what I ought to do in the morning."

She spoke in the most measured and deliberate way. It was plain she did not want to excite compassion. Her manner went so far as to imply that she would resent expressions of condolence. She seemed to wish the two men would regard her simply as an inexperienced woman confronted by an unexpected difficulty, and that they would confine themselves to the business aspect of the affair.

Santley and Paulton looked at one another inquiringly.

"It will be impossible for you to stay by yourself in this house to-night," said Paulton, who was completely subjugated by her regal beauty, her sudden misfortune, and her forlorn plight.

"But what am I to do?" she asked, turning to him. "It is too late or too early to look for ordinary help; and if I could get a person to come and stay with me, this place is not fit to receive any one."

Paulton was overwhelmed by this speech and the contemplation of the scene before him. Here was the most superb woman he had ever seen in his life alone in this house of chaos by night with the dead body of her husband, who had spoken to her but a few hours ago. She could not live here by herself till daylight. It would drive her mad, or would kill her. It would be little short of murder to leave her as she was. He could see plainly that her present calmness was artificial, and that when the need for self-restraint caused by the presence of two strangers was removed, she would break down utterly, collapse—in all likelihood die. He knew that when highly strung natures break down at all they break down more completely than any others. Then he knew that his father and mother were the most kind-hearted and neighbourly people alive, and that if they only heard of the hideous position in which this woman was, they would hasten to her assistance. No doubt the hour—it must now be past two— was most awkward ; but if it was awkward for the succourer, how much more awkward for any one in need of help.

All this ran through his mind in a moment. He resolved to act; then he spoke :

"Mrs. Davenport, my father and mother live close by, only a few houses off. I am sure they will be greatly pleased and take it as a kindness if you will come up there to-night. I could send down the coachman to stay here. He is a most good-natured and trustworthy man."

Dr. Santley gave Paulton a peculiar look, of which the latter could make nothing.

"What!" she said. "At such an hour! I could not think of it."

"I can assure you," persisted Paulton, "it will not cause any inconvenience. My mother does not in the least mind getting up. I am perfectly certain both my father and mother would be greatly displeased with me if I did not do everything in my power to induce you to come."

He glanced at Santley for encouragement, and again found the incomprehensible expression on the doctor's face.

She seemed to hesitate. She looked down at her soft, round arm lying on the table.

"It is most considerate of you to make me such an offer, and if I felt perfectly sure your mother would not regard it as a very inconvenient intrusion, I should be disposed to accept it."

"Believe me, Mrs. Davenport, I am not exaggerating in the slightest degree when I say that my mother would be displeased with me if I omitted any argument likely to influence you. I appeal to Dr. Santley. He will tell you that my mother is most sympathetic. What do you say, doctor?"

"I am sure I know of no one of kindlier nature than Mrs. Paulton," said the doctor.

The face of Santley was now expressionless, the eyes of Mrs. Davenport were fixed on him.

"I will go," she said, and rose. She walked slowly down the side of the table until she reached the elbow of the couch.

She bent over the drooped head, kissed the forward-leaning forehead, and then went back to the door, and as she left the room said : " I shall be ready immediately. I do not like to go upstairs. I have a cloak and bonnet in the hall. Please bring the light here a moment."

" Will you wait until I come back ? " said Paulton to Santley, as he passed him by carrying the lamp. " I will not be more than half-an-hour."

" I'll wait for you," said the doctor.

In a few seconds Paulton replaced the lamp on the table, and then Mrs. Davenport and he left the house.

As soon as the sound of their footfalls had died away, the doctor once more approached the recumbent figure.

" I wish," he thought, " Paulton had not been so enthusiastic in his invitation. As a rule, spasmodic asthma does not kill directly. A little chloroform is not a bad

thing in spasmodic asthma; but too much
chloroform is a bad thing, and there has
been too much here. Why, it's all over
the beard, and shirt, and waistcoat! She
looks as if she could do anything. I hope
this is not a case of foul play."

CHAPTER III.

HINTS OF EARLY HISTORY.

ALFRED PAULTON had not said too much of the kindliness of his father and mother. He left Mrs. Davenport in the drawing-room and knocked at his mother's door, and explained to both father and mother what had occurred, and the step he had taken in the matter. After expressions of surprise and horror at the tragedy at Crescent House, both applauded his action. Mrs. Paulton then told him to go down to the guest and say that she would follow him in a few minutes.

When he got back to the drawing-room

he found the widow where he had left her.
She was sitting in an easy-chair, her elbow
resting on a table, her head on her hand.
She raised her head as he entered. Otherwise she did not move.

"My mother is delighted you have
come," he said. "She will be here in a
few minutes. I see the fire has gone out.
I hope you do not feel the place very
cold?"

She looked at him with a stony stare.
Her brows were slightly raised, but around
her eyes the lids were strangely contracted.
The expression of the whole face was that
of one who suffered pain, but was not
giving attention to the pain. When she
spoke, her voice was dry and hard.

"It is most kind of your mother to
interest and trouble herself about a perfect
stranger. I do not feel cold, thank you."

The contraction round the eyes relaxed.
A look of intelligence alarmed came into

her eyes, and she asked, in a husky voice :

"Do you know anything of cases such as this? I mean, do you know anything of the law in such cases?"

"The law!" he said, "the law! In what way do you mean?"

"Oh," she cried, covering her face with her hands, "it is dreadful to think of—horrible! Can you not tell me," she pleaded, "if—if it will be necessary to have an——"

She paused and looked at him beseechingly.

"An inquest?"

"Yes."

"Certainly not," he answered promptly. With this beautiful woman before him it was shocking to think of the ordeal and details of an inquest. "Mr. Davenport was suffering from a disease of long standing; it had been particularly bad to-night,

and a violent paroxysm overcame him.
My friend, Dr. Santley, will make it
right, and you will be spared all pain
that can possibly be diverted from you."

"Thank you," she said, feebly; and
she threw herself back in her chair.

Nothing further was said until Mrs.
Paulton entered the room. The young
man introduced Mrs. Davenport to his
mother; then he left to rouse the coachman for the purpose of sitting up at
Crescent House. As soon as Paulton had
arranged this, he hastened back to Dr.
Santley.

"I came as quickly as I could, doctor.
That poor woman is in a dreadful state
of mind; she looks to me as if she were
losing her reason."

"H'm," said the doctor, who was sitting
on a chair by the lamp on the table,
and had been reading a newspaper he
had happened to have in his pocket. He

seemed thoughtful or sleepy; Paulton
was not a man of nice observation.

"Poor thing!" said the latter, com-
passionately; "she is not only in great
grief for the loss of her husband, but
was very uneasy about the suddenness
of his death."

"No wonder," said the doctor drily.

The younger man sat down on a chair
and regarded his companion with surprise.
He had known the other for years, and
had always taken him for a simple, sympathetic man. His tone now was one
of cynical distrust, although distrust of
what Paulton could not even guess. He
leant forward and peered into Santley's
face.

"I told her to make her mind quite
easy on the score of the future. You
understand what I mean?"

"She does not want an inquest?"

"Precisely."

"That is unfortunate, for I will not certify."

"What!" cried Paulton, leaning still farther forward, "you will not certify as to the cause of death? What do you mean?"

He shivered, and looked apprehensively at the body reclining on the couch.

"I don't know what the cause of death was."

"She said spasmodic asthma."

"A disease that very, very rarely kills."

"I thought that, on the contrary, it was most fatal."

"No. In a paroxysm of coughing, something in the head or chest may give way, but asthma itself does not kill."

An uneasy expression came into the young man's face, and, looking straight into the doctor's eyes, he said:

"And in this case what do you think killed?"

"It is impossible to say until after the inquest. I found on the floor this"—he held a bottle up in his hand. "It is a two-ounce bottle, empty; it contained chloroform. There is chloroform spilt all over the beard, shirt, and waistcoat."

"But perhaps the chloroform was administered for the relief of the dead man?"

"Perhaps so," said Santley, rising; "we shall find out all at the inquest. I'm off to bed now. Let nothing be stirred here. Good-night."

As Dr. Santley turned away from the gate of Crescent House, Paulton's coachman came up and the young man was relieved. He walked home straight and went to bed.

It was past four by this time, and after the excitement of the night there was little chance of the young man closing his eyes. His life up to this had been barren of

adventure, and here was he now plunged
into the middle of an affair which would
be town talk in twenty-four hours. It
was quite plain to him, from Santley's
manner, that the latter did not think
the man had died a natural death, and
it was almost as plain he did not think
it was a case of accidental poisoning or
suicide. Gradually, as time went by, it
seemed to narrow itself down to one
question : Did or did not that superb
woman——? But no ; the mere question
was a hideous libel ! He wished he could
go to sleep ; but sleep would not come.
He tossed and tumbled until he felt
feverish. In the heat and hurry of events
a few hours old he had not had time for
thought ; now he had time for thought,
but he did not want to think. True,
he had no personal interest in that silent
room out of which he had stepped a little
while ago, but it haunted him, and lay

before his imagination, lighted up with a fierce light which made every object in it stand out with painful sharpness.

While the actions of which he had been a spectator were going on at Crescent House, all had been confusion, chaos. Now every object was firmly defined by a hard, rigid line; every sound had a metallic ring; every motion went forward with mathematical deliberateness and precision. And over this scene of rigid forms and circumspect movement presided the woman, whose dark and lofty beauty had filled him with amazed reverence.

Murder! Could it be that murder had been done? There could be no doubt Santley thought so. Murder done by whom? Ugh! How he wished he had had nothing to do with that house; and yet, it was a privilege even to have seen her, to have heard her voice, to have done her a slight service. Above all, it was consoling to think she was now under this roof. If a fool knew how his thoughts were running now, that fool might think he was in love with this woman. In love! Monstrous! He would as soon think of falling in love with a sunset, a melody, a poem.

Oh, if he could only sleep! Why should he trouble himself about this matter? Santley said there would be an inquest. That would be trouble enough for him in all conscience. He, of course, would have to appear, although he scarcely knew how his evidence could be material.

It must be near six o'clock now. There was no good in staying in bed any longer; he would get up and go out for a walk. It was dawn, he felt feverish, and the air would refresh him.

He set off at a quick pace. The breeze was raw and cold. He felt physically invigorated, but his mental unrest had not abated. Do what he would he could not banish the scene of the night from his mind—he could not get rid of the awful suspicion Santley's words had given rise to. Over and over he told himself that even the doctor had not explicitly formulated that suspicion. Over and over again that suspicion would intrude upon his thoughts.

He did not return to the house until breakfast-time. At the suggestion of Mrs. Paulton, Mrs. Davenport was breakfasting in her own room, as she was tired and shaken. Alfred had to go over the whole story once more for his father, but he was careful not to say a word of the terrible hint thrown out by Santley.

The moment breakfast was over he left home, and, without having made up his mind as to whither he was going, found himself in front of Santley's house just as the doctor was stepping into his brougham bound for his morning visits.

"I say, doctor," he said, getting up close to the other, "what you let fall about that unfortunate affair at Crescent House kept me awake all night. You really don't think there has been anything wrong?"

Santley shook his head gravely as he got into his brougham, saying:

"I don't know, Mr. Paulton; I can't say. But I am sorry you mixed yourself up with the affair more than was absolutely necessary."

This was but poor comfort to the young man. He found it impossible to believe any evil of that marvellous-looking woman. If there was anything in what Santley said it plainly pointed at her; for were not she and her husband the only people in the house?

He did not care to go home. He could
not meet that woman while even the hint
of such a suspicion was in his head. He
did not suspect her; but the suspicion had
been spoken to him, it was sounding in his
ears, and he could not bring himself to
stand face to face with her and hear that
murmur. He told himself this was an
absurd condition of mind; but he could
not help it. What was she to him, or he
to her, that he should thus give way to
such feelings? She was a beautiful, a
surprisingly beautiful woman to whom he
had rendered a slight service, shown a little
kindness. That was all.

He wandered aimlessly about for an hour,
and finally went into town. Dulwich was
intolerable to him. At Victoria railway
station he took a hansom and drove to
the Robin Hood Club. It was now between eleven and twelve. The club had
not been long open, and there were only

three members in the place. One of these happened to be Jerry O'Brien, a young Irishman, an intimate friend of Paulton, reputed to be clever, and known to be indolent. To him Paulton told the story of Crescent House, and what Dr. Santley had hinted at.

Up to this Jerry O'Brien had given little close attention to the story. He was smoking in a huge easy-chair with eyes half shut. The idea that a woman had poisoned her husband roused even him to attention, and as Paulton had finished his story he began to ask questions.

"And so this doctor of yours won't certify as to the cause of death, and thinks your goddess may have had a hand in it?"

"Yes. Isn't it horrible?"

"What is your goddess like?"

"Dark and most lovely. A noble kind of beauty."

" Good figure ? "

" Perfect."

" Did you hear her name ? "

" Yes ; Davenport."

Jerry O'Brien blew the smoke of his cigar away with a whistle.

" Is she English ? "

" No. I think Scotch."

" Possibly Irish ? "

" Ay, she may be Irish."

" And her husband was an elderly man, with a greyish full beard and chronic asthma ? "

" Yes. Do you know them ? "

" By heavens, I do ! And I think I know, if there has been foul play, who cheated."

" Who ? Not she ? "

" Not she directly, any way, but Tom Blake, the biggest scoundrel Ireland has turned out for years and years, and an old lover of hers. I saw him in Piccadilly to-day. He looked as if he was meditating murder. Poor old Davenport!—I knew him well. He was a simple man. She must have told Blake of the lonely house. Your doctor is right. There is reason for suspicion, and I'll be at the inquest. You will, of course?"

"Unfortunately, yes."

"Then I promise you will hear an interesting story."

Paulton shuddered.

CHAPTER IV.

SEEKING HELP.

YOUNG Paulton felt anything but relieved or cheered by Jerry O'Brien's words. He began now to feel it would have been wiser if he had not meddled in this affair. It was quite true his father and mother were the kindest couple in England; but, like most other middle-class elderly people, they were careful about appearances and preferred a smooth and easy way of life to one of surprises and startling situations.

And now were they—owing to his hasty action of the night before—brought

into immediate contact with an inquest
and a story, which might turn out to be
a scandal, which might have for its core
an infamous crime. This other man, this
Blake, of whom Jerry O'Brien spoke in
such unmeasured terms, might, if he appeared upon the stage, complicate matters
infinitely.

Besides, although he had taken elaborate
care to tell himself he was in no danger
of falling in love with Mrs. Davenport,
that did not make it desirable a former
and disreputable admirer should be in
the neighbourhood. But, after all, Jerry
O'Brien's surmises might be quite base-
less. This old admirer might have ceased
to admire—might never in all his life
have been within miles of Half Moon
Lane, the Crescent House.

At present what was he to do with
himself? There was a kind of treason
in leaving all the burden of the situation

on the shoulders of his father and mother.
He did not know anything about inquests
beyond what he had gathered now and
then from reading a summarised report
in a newspaper. If it was mean to keep
away from his father and mother, what
could he think of leaving this newly-
made widow derelict? And yet what
about this old lover? Confound the
whole thing! Now he was heartily sorry
he had bound himself up in it.

And yet when he thought of her
he charged himself with cowardice for
flinching.

"Look here, O'Brien," he said at length,
"what ought I to do?"

"Do!" cried O'Brien scornfully; "why,
get out of it as fast as ever you can.
I hope you're not such a fool as to mix
yourself and your family any more up in
this miserable matter."

Alfred shook his head gravely.

"I can't retreat now. I have promised to see her out of the trouble——"

"And a pretty chance you have of seeing her out of the trouble! My belief is that every hour will make matters only worse."

"Do be reasonable and try and help me. You know I would depend on you more than on any other man living. I can't go home and turn this woman out of doors, and you ought to be able to understand that I don't like to confess to the old people I have been hasty or unwise. Don't desert me, O'Brien."

The other got out of his chair with a growl, and began pacing up and down the smoking-room of the club. O'Brien had private reasons of his own for wishing to keep friendly with Alfred Paulton. Jerry knew no pleasanter house in all London to spend a long evening in than the Paultons', and he knew no nicer girl

in all London than Madge Paulton,
Alfred's younger sister. But these facts
were both reasons for his impatience with
his friend. He felt a firm conviction
the adventure of the night before would
have no gratifying sequel. The sight of
Tom Blake, taken in conjunction with
Paulton's story, was enough to make any
prudent man cautious. And here now
was Alfred, plunged headlong into one
of the most disagreeable experiences which
could befall a quiet-going citizen. It was
too bad, but there was no cure for the
thing. It would certainly be rather mean
of Alfred to retire from the position in
which he had voluntarily placed himself
with this woman. O'Brien could not
abandon his friend any more than his
friend could abandon this woman.

He stopped in his walk, and said,
abruptly:

"The first thing is to get a solicitor.
Do you know of one?"

"There's Spencer, my own man, or there's my father's."

"And a nice pair they'd make in a case of this kind. Your father's man wouldn't touch it with a forty-foot ladder, and Spencer would get every one connected with the matter locked up. No, you want a man that's accustomed to the work. He must be as sharp as bayonets and as persevering. I would not attach so much importance to this point, only that I know Tom Blake is about. I feel you are standing on a mine, and may be blown sky-high any moment. I have it! You must get Pringle—Pringle, of Pringle, Pringle, and Co. Young Pringle is the very man for you, and he's a good sort too. Come on, and I'll introduce you to him."

The two friends left the club and proceeded at once to the office of Pringle, Pringle, and Co. Here they were fortunate in finding the younger Pringle, and at their service.

He was a low-sized, stoutish, horsey-looking, clean-shaven man of about thirty-five, in very tight-fitting clothes. He bade the two visitors be seated, and then listened with exemplary patience to Paulton's story. When it was finished, he crossed his legs and reflected for a few moments.

"I see," he said—"I see. Supposing Mrs. Davenport is willing I should appear for her, I think all will be right. Of course, it would be nonsense to pretend to believe that a thing of this kind is agreeable. It is not. Things of this kind are awkward and painful; but that is all. I feel fully persuaded, beyond the inconvenience of appearing as a witness, Mrs. Davenport will suffer none. Your doctor must be mad, I should say, Mr. Paulton. You don't think he could be induced to certify?"

"I am perfectly sure he won't. I have known him some years, and he is a man of great determination," said Paulton.

"Well, we must only try and do the best we can. Has the deceased any relatives—blood relatives, I mean?"

"I don't know," said Paulton.

"Yes, he has a brother, who lives in the south of Ireland," answered O'Brien. "Mr. Davenport was somewhat peculiar in his thoughts and habits, but his brother is an oddity."

"Ah, that is not fortunate. No doubt he will want to know all about this unlucky affair.

"And now, O'Brien, it is your turn. I want you to tell me all you know about this other man, Blake."

"Well, I'll tell you all I know about the whole thing," said Jerry O'Brien.

"Ay, do," said the solicitor, settling himself comfortably in his elbow chair.

"The man who is dead, Louis Davenport, was a native of the south of Ireland, County Waterford, to be exact. His wife is about thirty-four, and he must have been about sixty when he died. She, too, is Irish; her maiden name was Butler. She comes of a good Cork family—the Butlers of Scrouthea. They were as poor as church mice. Davenport was rich, and had money, not land; and Marion Butler was a beauty, as my friend Paulton has told you.

"About ten years ago, when Louis Davenport was elderly, and Marion Butler no longer very young, he proposed to her father for her. The father was delighted, for Davenport promised all sorts of comfortable things about money; but when the matter was spoken of to Miss Butler, they found a difficulty had to be faced, for Mr. Tom Blake stood in the way.

"This Tom Blake is and was one of the

most hopeless scamps in Europe. He is
now about thirty-eight years of age, and
has deserved hanging for every year of his
life. He was in the army, to start with;
he was kicked out of it. He tried the Turf
for a while, until he was kicked out of that
too. Then he turned his hand to card-
sharping. What he's doing now, I don't
know, except he may have gone in for a
little murder. He's quite capable of it,
I assure you, Pringle—quite capable of it."

"And you say this Miss Butler had a
strong predilection for this objectionable
man ?"

"It amounted to nothing short of infatuation. As the account of the matter
reached me, she was assured by people
who were quite disinterested that he was
a thorough scamp. They might as well
have saved their breath. She would
listen to all they had to say, and simply
shake her head."

"And how did they in the end over come this infatuation?"

"They never overcame it at all. They got her to marry Davenport by appealing to the baseness of Blake's nature. Some friends of mine were very intimate with the Butlers at that time, and I heard the whole history of his abominable conduct. He was then in great extremities for money, and took a sum down to leave the country and hold no communication with her. That's the sort of man Tom Blake is."

"But surely this woman whom he treated so vilely cannot care for him still —cannot have any regard for such a scurvy knave?"

"I don't know how matters have gone of late. I have been out of their tracks for some time. If he has any influence now it may rest on fear, not fascination. I am quite sure if there is anything wrong, he is at the bottom of it. I have been in London for months now, and never saw him or heard of him. Is it a mere coincidence that I should come across him just as I hear this story from Paulton?"

"It is strange. I presume Mrs. Davenport is childless?"

"Yes. And as far as I know she is now absolutely alone in the world, if you do not count this brother-in-law, with whom she never got on well."

"I'll go out to Dulwich with you myself now. I think that will be the best thing."

The three men rose and walked to Ludgate Hill railway station.

CHAPTER V.

PRINGLE UNANSWERED.

WHEN the three men arrived at Dulwich, they went straight to Carlingford House, where Mr. Paulton lived. The owner was in. Some years ago he had retired from business in the City, and now interested himself in local affairs, his garden, his horses, and reading. He was bluff, white-haired, stout, brief of speech, straightforward, kindly. He was not quite sixty yet, notwithstanding his white hair.

Just as they got into the house he was crossing the hall. He paused, and held out his hand cordially to Jerry O'Brien.

"What lucky wind has blown you here at such an hour?" he cried. "You are just too late for luncheon; but I dare say they'll be able to find something for you and Alfred, and——"

He now became aware the third man was a stranger, and stopped.

Young Paulton introduced the solicitor, and then all four went into a little library on the right hand side of the hall. Alfred felt acutely the difficulty of his position, and he found himself completely at a loss to explain the situation to his father. Then it occurred to him to appeal to O'Brien for help.

"Jerry," said he, "tell the governor all about it."

The old man looked apprehensively from one to the other. There was evidently something wrong.

"Out with it whatever it is, my lad," said he to O'Brien, and, without further delay, Jerry began. When he had finished, the old man seemed thunderstruck. It was incredible that he should ever be brought into contact with such people, and such a history. He had sat down in an easy-chair, and now he felt he had not the strength to get out of it. He looked blankly around at the three figures and the bookcases and the walls, as if he were awaiting contradiction from animate or inanimate objects. But no one spoke, and nothing occurred to reassure him.

At last the solicitor came forward with, "You know, sir, we have really nothing whatever to go on yet. Dr. Santley's dissatisfaction and the lady's shrinking from an inquiry, and the presence of this man Blake in London may all point to nothing —end in nothing. I have come out here to clear up the whole thing, and I have no doubt that if I might be favoured with half-an-hour's conversation with Mrs. Davenport all our uneasiness would disappear."

A look of hope came into Mr. Paulton's face. He rose, and, approaching the solicitor, said: "I wish you would see her and bring us good news. She is keeping her room, but I think she will come down to the drawing-room if Mrs. Paulton asks her. You would greatly oblige me if you would see her. I wouldn't be mixed up with a case of that kind for any consideration."

"I shall be only too happy to do anything I can in your interest, which is, I presume, identical with that of the afflicted lady. The first step to be taken is to ascertain through Mrs. Paulton if Mrs. Davenport will see me."

"I'll go immediately." Mr. Paulton moved towards the door.

"A moment, sir. Don't you think that

if Mrs. Davenport will see me it would be as well Mrs. Paulton said a few words of preparation. Such as, for instance, that in cases of this kind it was always desirable to have advice, and to allow some one to act instead of the principal; as owing to the distress attendant on loss one is little able to look after matters of detail. If Mrs. Paulton would be good enough she might say that you thought I might be of some slight use. Anything of that kind Mrs. Paulton might say would prevent my coming too suddenly on the widow."

"Quite so. I am glad you mentioned it. I shall do exactly as you suggest. I shall be back as soon as I can." He hurried out of the room.

In less than a quarter of an hour he returned, rubbing his hands. It was plain by his appearance that he had been successful. Yes; Mrs. Davenport was in the drawing-room, and would see Mr. Pringle.

He went up, was introduced by Mrs. Paulton, who then retired, leaving client and lawyer together.

The lady had sent up to Crescent House for a change of clothes, and now appeared in a plain, black dress, with sleeves of ordinary length, and without the orange scarf or the diamonds at her throat or girdle. She motioned him to a seat, and then took one herself.

What Alfred said had prepared him for something out of the common, but for nothing like what he now saw. He was prepared to meet a beautiful woman in need of his help—he found a regal woman who might perhaps condescend to give him orders. Her face was absolutely without colour, save the full red lips, the dark impenetrable eyes, and the black eyebrows. But the modelling of the face was superb, and the carriage of the head magnificent. And yet he was conscious of

something that detracted from, or contra-
dicted the imperial grandeur of the head.
There was no splendour in the pose of the
figure.   In the arms, and figure, and gait,
there was an air of patient, suppliant
dutifulness, that seemed to plead for love
and protection.

"Mrs. Paulton has explained to me,"
she said, in a low, soft voice, "that it is
better I should have some one to advise
me in the present circumstances, and that
you have been good enough, Mr. Pringle,
to allow me to look to you for the help I
need."

She spoke with great precision and
delicacy of tone.   It was a flattery to
hear her utter one's name.

He answered in a low voice.   His voice
never before seemed so harsh in his own
ears.   "It is well for you to have
advice.   You may rely upon my doing all
I can for you."

It was simply monstrous to associate this woman with the idea of crime. Attorney and man of the world though he was, he could not be persuaded into such a ridiculous belief. O'Brien must be a fool. Or no, it wasn't O'Brien—it was Paulton's doctor who had the honour of broaching that absurdity.

"I am quite sure of that. And the first thing I want to ask you about is, when I shall need your advice?—for I know absolutely nothing about such things. Mr. Davenport has a brother living; I suppose he had better be telegraphed for?"

"Yes. He must be telegraphed for at once."

"Then I suppose the—funeral must be arranged for immediately?"

"Yes. Then, as you are aware, a few legal formalities have to be gone through before that."

"What are they?"

"Have you not been told?"

"No. Pray tell me."

"Well, the sad event took place so suddenly that a certain form has to be observed. In this case it will be the merest form."

"Some sort of certificate has to be got, I dare say?"

"Well, yes; if you put it in that way."

"And what must I do?"

"You say you know nothing of such matters as we are now talking about. The first advice I have to give you is, that you must repose full confidence in me. Remember, I am bound by a rule of my profession to respect any confidence you may place in me. I shall have to ask you questions which would be impertinent from any one but your legal adviser. Mind, all this is merely to save you annoyance hereafter. Will you trust me with the history of last night?"

"I will—as far as I may," faintly.

"I have heard something of last night. I will not trouble you with any inquiries that I do not consider absolutely necessary. You and Mr. Davenport arrived together yesterday evening, and came on to your new house close by, your furniture having preceded you by only a few hours, so that the house was all in disorder?"

"Yes."

"And you came unaccompanied by any servant; may I ask you why was this?"

"Mr. Davenport had peculiar notions about never moving servants from one house to another. He insisted on getting new servants when we changed."

"So that it was at his desire you came unattended?"

"Certainly. Only it was too late when we arrived, we should have got some one to help us."

"And was Mr. Davenport in his

usual health when you reached Crescent House?"

"No. His asthma was worse, but not very much worse. When it was bad he could not lie down. My room was the only one in order, and he said he would rest on the couch for the night. I left him at about eleven, but did not go to bed, as I was not quite easy about him, and thought I'd come down and put some coal on the fire later. I fell asleep in a chair, and when I went down I found all was over."

"He had a large quantity of chloroform by him?"

"Yes; a two-ounce bottle, almost full."

"And he was in the habit of using chloroform when the spasms were bad?"

"Yes; but what do you mean? You are perplexing and terrifying me. Pray speak plainly to me."

"I shall very soon be done. Remember,

I told you I should ask no question that was not absolutely essential. Now, from the time you and Mr. Davenport entered that house, and until Mr. Paulton and the doctor entered it, had any other person access to it?"

She grasped the edge of the table near her. She trembled as in an ague. Her lips grew as pallid as her brow. She did not speak.

"Remember, anything you communicate is privileged, and will not find its way abroad through me. I am trying to get the means of protecting you. Of course you are fully at liberty to refuse to answer me now; but all questions will have to be answered at the inquest."

"Inquest!" she whispered, in a voice of abject terror. She rose to her feet and stood swaying to and fro, one hand still grasping the table. "Inquest! Mr.

Paulton said there would be no inquest. There *shall* be no inquest."

"The bottle was found *empty.*"

"Oh, Heaven, take away my life from me!"

"Was Blake in the house that night?"

She took her hand from the table and stood still a moment, looking upward. Then slowly she raised both her arms aloft, and cried:

"Hear Thou my prayer!"

She stood a while motionless. After a moment she said, in a firm voice:

"No mercy!"

She dropped her arms to her side, bowed slowly to him, and then with erect head and a firm step walked out of the room.

CHAPTER VI.

HER SUDDEN RESOLVE.

FOR some time after Mrs. Davenport left the drawing-room, young Pringle stood motionless, with his hand resting on the back of a chair. The scene had taken him completely by surprise. At the beginning of it he had made up his mind, or rather his emotions had so wrought upon him, he determined she had no reprehensible connection with the event of the night before.

He had implored her to confide in him, and she had given him her confidence up to a certain point. Then she not only refused to trust him any more, but behaved in such an extraordinary way as to lay herself open to the gravest suspicions. If she had at the end of their interview fallen down in a faint, he could have formed an opinion of the case—an opinion which would not have been very favourable to her, but still something definite. But the manner of her leaving the room seemed to throw a new light, or rather cast a new kind of shadow on the case.

He had better go down at once and inform Mr. Paulton of what had occurred.

He left the drawing-room and returned to the library. In as few words as possible he told the owner of the house that he feared there was no chance of avoiding the unpleasantness of an inquest. Mr. Paulton then asked what the lady had said, but Pringle explained he could not divulge it. He made no comment whatever.

The old man breathed heavily, and looked about helplessly when the solicitor had finished.

The two young men returned his look, but there was no comforting assurance in their gaze.

Alfred Paulton was now profoundly impressed with a sense of the unpleasantness into which he had drawn the whole family.

"I am very sorry, sir," said he, addressing his father, "that I have been the cause of all this worry. Of course I had not the least idea last night that anything of this kind was likely to arise. If I had, I should never have acted as I did."

"It is most unfortunate," said the father.

"Well," broke in Jerry O'Brien, "there's

no use now in crying over spilt milk. What we have to ask ourselves is: How can it be best faced—eh, Pringle? Isn't that the practical question?"

"I think so," said the solicitor. "For my part I find myself in rather an awkward position. Mrs. Davenport's interests and yours, Mr. Paulton, can scarcely be said to be any longer identical. I cannot advise both. Besides, Mr. Paulton, you have a solicitor of your own. My position is uncomfortable—scarcely professional."

"My father's solicitor would be little or no use in this case, Mr. Pringle," said Alfred. "That is the reason we came to you."

"Mr. Pringle," said the father, "pray do not throw us over. If you do, I shall not know where to turn. Can you not show us any way out of this unhappy situation?"

"Of course," said Pringle, "you must

put up with the consequences of facts up to this moment. What I suppose you to be asking me is—How can further con- sequences be avoided, or can they be avoided at all?"

"Precisely," said Mr. Paulton. "Can they be avoided at all?—and if so, how?"

"Well, as you offered the hospitality of your roof to Mrs. Davenport, and she has accepted it, you can't say to her, or even show to her, that you wish her to go——"

"Quite impossible," interrupted Alfred.

"But might I not say—that supposing she will see me again—a thing I doubt very much—it would be most desirable for her to move into town, so that she might be near me and I near her?"

"That would not be a bad plan," said Mr. Paulton, looking at his son and O'Brien for confirmation. "What do you think, boys?"

"I don't see what better can be done," said O'Brien, answering for the two.

He answered quickly, for he was half afraid that Alfred had not even yet made up his mind as to the desirability of her leaving the house.

"The great difficulty is that time is short, and I don't think I could intrude upon her again to-day. We had quite a scene upstairs. Judging from the state of agitation in which she left me, I should imagine she will not see any one on business during the remainder of the day."

At that moment the door of the library opened and Mrs. Davenport stepped into the room. She was in her walking dress.

All the men rose and stood looking at her silently. Mr. Paulton was the first to recover his presence of mind, and offered her a chair.

She came over quietly to where he stood, bowing slightly as she moved.

"I hope I do not disturb you, gentlemen," she said, in a gentle voice and with a wan smile.

"Not in the least," said Mr. Paulton. "Will you not take a chair?"

"Thank you, no. I am going out."

"Going out! May not some one go for you—one of my daughters or one of the servants?"

"You are very good; but I must go myself. I have just been explaining to Mrs. Paulton. I have come, Mr. Paulton, to thank you for your great kindness to me, a complete stranger. Believe me, I shall never forget it—never as long as I live. If a friend in need is a friend indeed, you have been a great friend; for I never wanted a friend more than I did this morning. I have come to thank you and to say good-bye."

"Good-bye!" he cried in astonishment. "Why should you leave us?"

His surprise was not feigned.

"Since you were kind enough to give me shelter, a serious difference has arisen in my position. When I came into your house I believed that there would be no unusual trouble about my poor husband's death. Now I understand in that I was mistaken. It would be monstrous on my part to involve you, Mr. Paulton, in any way in this unpleasantness, and it will be best for me to be alone."

She spoke with perfect composure, and Pringle could scarcely believe that this calm, collected woman, with the wan smile and resigned air, was the one who, a little while ago, had spoken impassioned words of despair.

Mr. Paulton was disturbed by this sudden and unexpected prospect of deliverance. There could be no doubt of the woman's sincerity. Here she was, without a suggestion from any one, offering to take the very step he desired. It was necessary to say something, and kind-hearted as he was, a polite lie was a sin utterly beneath him. He felt extremely awkward.

"Since you consider it useful to your own interest that you should go, I will say nothing against your leaving us."

"Allow me, Mrs. Davenport, to say that I think it will be better for you to be in London than here. I can then see you at any moment without delay," joined in Pringle.

When she heard his voice she turned to him. A shadow passed across her face. When he ceased speaking, she merely bowed. Turning her glance once more on Mr. Paulton, she went on:

"I have explained matters to Mrs. Paulton, and said good-bye to her. Your daughters are out, but your wife has promised me to say good-bye to them for me; and now there remains for me to say good-bye to only you and your son."

She held out her hand.

The host suffered a revulsion of feeling now that he heard her say good-bye, and saw her hold out her hand to him. It was hard to picture this beautiful woman alone in London, with her new woe. As long as she was an abstraction, as long as she was upstairs, and he regarded her as simply the source of notoriety if not of scandal, it was easy to wish her away at any inconvenience to herself or cost to him. But here she was now anticipating his wishes, doing precisely as he had most desired—about to launch herself alone on the vast ocean of London without a friend, and that, too, at the very time when she was most in need of friendly countenance and protection. It was too bad—much too bad.

He took her hand, and said, with perfect sincerity now:

"I am really sorry to say good-bye to you—really sorry you must go. I would like to be of any service to you I can. Will you, as a favour, promise me, if I can in any way assist you, you will let me know?"

"I will, indeed, Mr. Paulton. I am most grateful to you, and I am sure you would do anything you could for me; but"—she paused and sighed—"I am greatly afraid no one can do much to help me now. I must make up my mind to bear what cannot be avoided—to bear it bravely."

The tone in which these words were uttered and the smile which accompanied them were worse than any tears.

"But," said Mr. Paulton, still keeping the hand she had given him, "do you not

think you had better wait a little, until
evening, even if no longer?"

"I am greatly obliged to you.   But
what is to be gained by delay? Nothing."

"Well, but where do you propose
going? What hotel do you intend staying at?"

"I know one," she answered, wearily,
as she withdrew her hand gently from
his.   "It does not matter which or
where."

"But you are not taking anything
with you! You cannot go merely as you
are!"

"I fear I must. I cannot take anything out of that awful house—no, never"
—with a shudder. "All the things that
are now there are like my dead husband
—dead to me for ever. I can get what I
need in London."

"At all events, you must not go alone.
You must allow some one to escort you.

I am certain my son would be delighted to take you wherever you may wish to go."

" It would give me great pleasure," said Alfred eagerly.

" You are both, I know, too good and kind to mistake for ungraciousness the refusal which I must give to your offer. I have no alternative but to go alone."

" Mrs. Davenport," said Pringle, " I am going to town at once. May I hope you will allow me to see you as far as either Ludgate Hill or Victoria? I am afraid that my want of caution when speaking to you a few minutes ago upstairs may have betrayed me into saying or implying more than I really should. We could talk a little more on the way in."

" With your permission, I will go by myself. Farewell ;" and, with a bow that included all, she left the room.

They saw her walk through the little

garden, open the gate, and reach the road. Then they lost sight of her.

For a long while no one spoke. Mr. Paulton broke the silence. "I'm very sorry." He did not say for what; he scarcely knew for what.

"She's a wonderful woman," said Jerry O'Brien. "I am not surprised at her not speaking to me. She bowed to me as much as to say she knew me. I often met her before, but never saw her in any humour like this. Why, in the name of all that's mysterious, would she not allow any one to go with her? It could not do her any harm for either you or Pringle or Alfred to go with her."

"That struck me as most strange," said Mr. Paulton.

"We are all friends here," said Pringle. "It doesn't seem strange to me. It seems foolish, though. If they want her they can catch her abroad as well as in England."

" Abroad ! " said Mr. Paulton, in perplexity. " Surely she is not going abroad
before the funeral of her husband. No
woman would think of leaving the country
before her husband is buried."

" Under certain circumstances, a woman
might if *an inquest* was to precede the
burial."

" Oh, I see."

" Now, gentlemen, I think we ought to
be able to guess why she would have no
luggage, no escort. She is going to disguise
herself and fly to the Continent."

CHAPTER VII.

LIGHT AFTER DARKNESS.

WHEN Mrs. Davenport left Paulton she walked straight to Herne Hill railway station. She asked when the next train would start for Victoria, and having learned there would be one in ten minutes, she took a ticket for that terminus, and then sat down on one of the seats on the platform.

It was cold, raw, dull, rainless February weather, and she was lightly clad, but she did not mind that. Her thoughts were turned inward, and she had but a dimly reflected idea of things surrounding her.

When the train steamed into the station, she rose in a quick but mechanical way, and took her seat in an empty compartment. Upon arriving at Victoria, she left the train in the same quick, mechanical way, got into a cab, and drove to a house in Jermyn Street. Having engaged a bed-room and sitting - room here, she sat down at once and wrote a letter.

As soon as the letter was finished she left the house, dropped the letter into the first post-pillar, and then ascended to the middle section of Regent Street. She visited several shops, bought many things, and ordered many more. When this was done she paused, seemingly at a loss.

"My letter," she thought, "will not be there until night. In the meantime, what shall I do?" She walked slowly down Regent Street. At last she started. "How stupid," she thought, "I have

been not to telegraph! If I had telegraphed I could have had an answer in
an hour."

She hastened forward, asked a policeman
where the nearest telegraph office was, and
on arriving there despatched a message.
Then she went back to Jermyn Street,
and, laying aside her bonnet and mantle,
waited.

In an hour and a half a reply came. It
ran :

"*I shall be with you almost as soon as
this.*"

When she read the message she got up
and walked about the room in a state of
great excitement. It was now dark, and
the gas had not yet been lighted in the
room. As she paced up and down she
wrung her hands and moaned. After a
while she became calmer, but still con-

tinued walking up and down. She had eaten nothing that day, yet she felt no want of food. In fact, when the servant, upon her return, suggested that she had better order dinner, she had refused to do so with a shudder. She knew she should need for the coming interview all her strength, but she could not bear the notion of food. She had not slept during the whole night, yet she felt no want of sleep.

"I feel," she thought, "as though my sorrows were immortal, and that I shall require earthly succour no more."

She had not long to wait in solitude. A hansom drove up to the door, a man jumped out, and in a few minutes he was ushered into the room. He found her still in the dark, leaning on the mantel-shelf.

"Marion," he said — "are you here, Marion?"

"Yes," she answered, "I am here."

"I cannot see you, it is so dark."

"It is very dark. It never has been darker in all my life, and you know it."

"Will you not shake hands with me and order lights?"

"Neither. What is to be said can best be said in the dark. It is in the nature of darkness itself. Sit down. I prefer to stand; I wish you to sit. Sit down."

His eyes were now becoming accustomed to the obscurity. He found a chair, and sat down.

"Are you alone?" he asked, looking up at where she stood, motionless, by the mantelpiece.

"*Absolutely,*" she answered, in a cold, hard voice. "And you know it."

"How could I know it? I got your telegram, and came at once. Marion, you are speaking to me in a tone I am unused to from you."

"Ay," she said, "I am unused to my own voice in its present tone. I am risking much for you, and you do not deserve that I should risk anything for you."

"Marion," he cried, half-rising, "you have not left him? You have not resolved to throw your fate in with mine at last? Marion, my darling! Marion, let me come to you."

"Stay where you are," she said, in a tone of perplexity, and with a shudder. "If you move from that chair, it must only be for the door. Remember this once for all."

"You are very hard, Marion—very hard. It is a long day since we met, and now you will not even give me your hand. You would give your hand to the most ordinary friend you have: think of what we were once."

His voice had a firm, manly, straightforward ring in it, and withal an undertone of passionate entreaty.

"I have thought too much of what has been once. I have thought too much of what was between you and me long ago. I have another matter to think of to-night."

"And what is that, Marion?"

"I have to think of last night."

He uttered a cry of surprise and half rose from his chair.

"Did you know I was there? I thought you were asleep. He said you were. Did he tell you I was there?"

She paused a moment and made a powerful effort to control herself. When she spoke, her voice was unsteady, and showed that a violent conflict was going on in her breast.

"He told me nothing," she said. "I have sent for you in order that you may tell me all. Now go on. All, remember."

"All?" he asked. "I would rather not tell you all. I never told you a lie yet."

"All," she said—"all, or go."

He shifted uneasily for a few minutes on his chair, and then spoke:

"Well, Marion, since you will have it all, you shall. I am no better than ever I was. I leave it to you to say if I could, being only human, be much worse. You might have made a different man of me once. You wouldn't. Let that pass."

"Yes, let that pass, and let it pass quickly. I did not sell you for a sum of money."

Her voice was scornful.

"No, you did not. You did better.

You sold yourself for a sum of money. Shall we cry truce?"

"Yes; go on."

"I've been a good deal on the Continent. I've been doing a great many things I should not do. Amongst others, I have been gambling; and, worst of all, I have lost. There are many excuses for a man gambling. There is no excuse for a man losing. Well, I got cleaned out, and I came home—I mean I went back to Ireland.

"Naturally I faced south. Naturally I went on to Waterford. Naturally I found myself in Kilcash."

She made a gesture of dissent. But it was too dark for him to see. She said: "Most unwise and most unnatural."

"It may have been unwise, but it was most natural. What can be more natural than that a man should go where his heart—— But if I say any more in this strain, you will be angry?"

"Most assuredly."

"Well, when I got to Kilcash, I kept my ears open, and soon I heard that you were about to leave Kilcash House and take a house in or near London. I inquired still further, found out the day you were to leave, and got the address of the house you had taken. I came on to London.

"I arrived here the night before last. I knew you could not be in your new house until late in the day. I wanted to call most particularly. There was not an hour to be lost. It was neck or nothing with me. I resolved to call at Crescent House that very night, and I did."

"You did?" she said, in a voice like a terrified echo.

"You knew I was there. He told you?"

"No; go on. Go on, I say. You did not ask for me?"

"No. I wanted to see him."

"It was close to eleven, or after it then?"

"After it."

"And you wanted to see him at such an hour, and you knew he was an invalid?" she said, scornfully.

"I was an invalid myself."

"You! What was the matter with you?"—again that tone of scorn.

"A worse disease than his—poverty."

"What!" she cried, leaving the mantelpiece, and going a step towards him in the dark. "I thought you got the price of your—of *me* before."

"Marion, you are unjust—cruelly unjust. When I called on your husband last night, it was not to *beg* or to try and get money

from him, because of anything in which you
or I ever took part. I had a claim with
which you have no connection, and the
nature of which I will not divulge to you.
He may if he likes."

"He never will," she said, with something between a laugh and a sob.

"So be it. It may be all the better the
matter should never be spoken of. But
to proceed. I knocked and he let me in.
He explained that you were gone to bed,
and that he and you were alone in the
house. He was very polite, for he had an
idea of why I came—or rather of the card
of introduction, so to speak, that I brought
with me. He made me take a chair, told
me he was not well enough to lie down, as
he had one of his bad attacks of asthma,
though by no means a very bad one, and
we had a pleasant general conversation for
half-an-hour or so."

"Pleasant conversation!" she cried, falling back to her old position at the chimney-piece.

"Yes, I assure you it was quite a pleasant conversation. He told me all the incidents of your journey over from Ireland, and I amused him with my experiences on the Continent."

"This is too ghastly," she said. "Do not tell me any more about it. Did he give you—what you came for?"

"Oh, yes, or part of it."

"And then?" she asked, in a hard, constrained voice.

"And then after a few more words I stood up and said good-bye, left the house, and came back to town."

"Wait," she said. "I will give you another chance. Sit where you are. I shall be back in a few minutes."

"In the dark?" he asked.

"Yes. Is there anything in the dark that frightens you?"

"No," he answered; "but it is stupid to sit in the dark alone."

"Perhaps when I am gone you may not be quite alone. You may have memories for company."

There was great meaning in her voice.

He said merely "Perhaps," and she was gone.

While she was away he sat perfectly still. There was little or no light from the dull low fire, and as the blinds were down and curtains drawn, none reached the room from the street.

In a few minutes he heard the door open and some one enter. She came to her old position by the chimney-piece and said :

"Now, if you can find a match, you may light the gas."

He had wax cigar-lights in his pocket. He struck one, and in a moment the gas flared up. He looked at her, and cried, starting back :

"Merciful heavens, Marion, what masquerade is this!"

"No masquerade," she said calmly, scrutinizing him. "These are my widow's weeds come from the mourning warehouse a few minutes ago. They say you ought to be prepared to see me in them."

"I—I!—prepared to see you in widow's weeds! Is Davenport dead?"

"Women whose husbands are living do not wear such things as these. They say you ought to be prepared to see me dressed as I am now."

She touched the streamers of her cap and pointed to the crape of her dress.

"What do you mean by saying *they* say I ought to be prepared for this? Who are *they?*—and what do you mean?"

"As I left the room a moment ago, a servant brought me this note. Read it."

He took the note and read it first quickly, a second time slowly. Then, letting it fall from his grasp, he threw his hands above his head, and crying out, " Oh, God !" fell back on a chair.

CHAPTER VIII.

SHORTLY after Mrs. Davenport left Carlingford House, Half Moon Lane, that afternoon, a supplementary luncheon was announced, and the four men went into the dining-room.

Mr. Paulton had already lunched with the family, but he wished to be with the others; so he sat down at the table with them, and broke a biscuit and half-filled a glass with sherry. Jerry O'Brien and Pringle were in no humour for trifling with food; they were both downright hungry. Alfred ate mechanically, and was much pre-occupied. The talk, therefore, for a quarter of an hour, was slight, fragmentary, as though by some agreement: no one referred to what had just occurred in the library, or to anything else connected with Crescent House. Young Pringle felt that although there must be and are extremely interesting tragedies in the world, luncheon, when one is hungry, was a matter not to be neglected. He had more than once in a criminal court eaten sandwiches and drunk sherry in the interval for luncheon, with the moral certainty that his client, who had been temporarily removed from the dock, would be sentenced to death before the Court rose, and hanged before that day four weeks.

Here were a cold rabbit pie, cold ham, and excellent sherry, well-baked, fine white bread, and nicknacks, and no particular reason for hurry—no fear of hearing "Silence" called out while one was but

half-finished. The day was dull, but there
was an ample fire burning brightly in the
grate, the chair was soft and well-designed,
so why should he bother himself for another
quarter of an hour?

It was very easy for him to hold his
tongue and to assure himself that he need
not bother himself just now about Mrs.
Davenport and her unpleasant predicament;
but her predicament would not be banished,
and every now and then some incident of
either the drawing-room or library interview would rush into his mind with all
the unexpected suddenness of that unwelcome cry of "Silence!" in the middle
of luncheon at a criminal trial.

Upon the whole, that luncheon was not
as calm or as successful as young Pringle
meant it to be. He had never seen any
one at all like Mrs. Davenport before, and
he could make little or nothing of her.
He now began to think that he had talked

flippantly when he said she was certainly about to leave the country. Reviewing all he had seen and heard, he came to the conclusion that the safest thing for him to assume at present was—nothing. At length he spoke, addressing Alfred and Jerry O'Brien:

"Although Mrs. Davenport did not say anything to the effect when leaving, I suppose I had better act for her—until I hear something to the contrary."

Jerry O'Brien glanced at Alfred, and saw what he wished to say, but held back from speaking, because of the trouble his hasty action of the night before had brought about. Therefore Jerry made himself spokesman for his friend.

"Of course, Pringle, you go on acting for her, on her behalf. She has left this house finally now, and is not likely to cause any new unpleasantness here. Whether Mrs. Davenport is to blame or not, she

can't be left alone and unaided in such a
strait as this. What do you say, Mr.
Paulton ? "

"I am quite of your opinion, O'Brien.
Now that she is out of the house I would
be disposed to do anything I could for her.
It's different now from what it was an
hour ago. Go on, Mr. Pringle ; and I
most sincerely hope she may come out
of the inquiry without the shadow of
blame."

" I sincerely hope so," said Pringle,
rising. Luncheon was over by this time.
" Now, the first thing I should like, is
to have a look at the place—at this Crescent
House, as you call it."

Alfred and O'Brien got up, and in a
few minutes the three found themselves
in the hall of that house. The police were
already there.

Pringle told the officers who he was and
then proceeded to make inquiries. The

following was the state of affairs at that
time :

The inspector had been there about an
hour. He had made an elaborate, but
not exhaustive search in the room. The
body was in the position it had been found
in. An empty two-ounce bottle had been
discovered on the floor. This was the
bottle. It was labelled chloroform, smelt
of chloroform, and had no cork in it. A
cork which fitted it, and which also smelt,.
although faintly, of chloroform, had been
found on the table close by the body.

In the pockets of the deceased had been
discovered a number of letters, a small sum
of money, and a pocket-book. This was
the pocket-book. It was thin, and covered
with Russia leather; it was old, and had
been but little used. It contained several
addresses, and on the first leaf was written
a date of eleven years ago. It was more
than likely this date corresponded with

that on which the book became the property of deceased.

Most of the memoranda in that book could have no bearing on the present case, as most of them had evidently been made long ago. The last entry but one was dated in what was believed to be the handwriting of the deceased. It was made more than two years ago. After this last entry but one, a leaf was missing. A leaf had evidently been torn out—and clumsily torn out, too—for a jagged portion of the leaf remained behind.

Then came the last entry of all. This was also apparently in the handwriting of deceased. The writing was in pencil, and very shaky, and for a long time could not be deciphered. It was headed " Crescent House." The domicile fixed the date, for the night before was the only occasion on which Mr. Davenport crossed the threshold of that house. He had not even seen the house before renting it, but took it on the representation of an agent. The words on this page were :

"*Pretended death. Blake gone. He emptied chloroform on me—held me down. Can't stir. Dying.*"

After reading this the three men stood aghast for a while. They looked at one another. They looked at the inspector. The inspector shook his head.

"There's hangman's work here," he said ; and he was about to turn away, when a sudden thought struck Pringle. He said to the inspector :

"I beg your pardon. Does that pocket-book contain any London address of Mr. Davenport ?"

"I don't know," said the inspector; "and I am afraid I have already shown you too much."

"I'd be very much obliged to you if you'd see. I represent Mrs. Davenport in this matter, and at the moment I don't know where to find her. She omitted to give me her address when she left me this afternoon. I want to write to her, and if you find any London address of Mr. Davenport, I'll chance directing my letter there. That can do no harm to any one."

The inspector hesitated, but at length opened the pocket-book, and after a search, said :

"There's an address here at Jermyn Street ; but it's six years old."

"Never mind," said Pringle ; "I'll risk it. What is it ?"

The inspector read it out, and Pringle took it down.

Pringle, Alfred Paulton, and Jerry O'Brien were about to leave the room, when the first turned to the inspector, and said :

"By-the-way, you did not find the page that has been torn out of the pocket-book?"

"No," said the inspector, nodding his head significantly; "but there's evidence enough on what we *did* find to hang a score of men."

The three then walked to Herne Hill railway station, and took tickets for Ludgate. At the latter place Pringle left the two friends and went back to his office.

Here he sat down and wrote the following letter:

"Lincoln's Inn Fields, E.C.
"Feb. —, 18—.

"DEAR MADAM,

"By accident I got this address, and will chance writing you here in the hope this note may reach you.

"I have been to Crescent House. A

pocket-book of the late Mr. Davenport has been found. It contains the following entry in the handwriting of deceased: 'Pretended death. Blake gone. He emptied the chloroform on me—held me down. Can't stir. Dying.'

"Awaiting your further instructions,

"I am, dear Madam,

"Yours faithfully,

"RICHARD PRINGLE."

This was the note which Mrs. Davenport handed Thomas Blake as she stood over him in her fresh widow's weeds the night after her husband's death.

CHAPTER IX.

"WHICH OF US IS MAD?"

THE morning after the interview between Mrs. Davenport and Tom Blake in Jermyn Street, there were paragraphs about Mr. Davenport's death in the daily papers. These paragraphs were almost colourless, and barely suggested any cause for uneasiness. They all wound up by saying that the inquest would be held next day.

That afternoon Richard Pringle called on chance at the house in Jermyn Street, and found Mrs. Davenport at home. She received him in a dreamy, half-

conscious way, and answered listlessly
the common-place questions he put to
her. Before seeing her he had made up
his mind not to refer to the scene which
had taken place between them yesterday.
He was firmly convinced she would not
give him her full confidence, and that
to seek to get at the bottom of the
affair would be only to court obstruction.
From her manner he assumed she wished
nothing to be said of what had taken place
in the Paultons' drawing-room at Dulwich.
He began by trying to prepare her for
the inquest. She shuddered slightly when
he used that word, and yet seemed but in-
differently alive to the importance of the
situation. She answered in monosyllables,
and contented herself mostly with merely
bowing her head in token that she attended
to what he said.

No material advantage could be gained
by speaking of the former interview

between them. He had drawn his own
conclusions from it, and it was abundantly
clear to him she wished that interview
ignored. Now that he was once more
under the spell of her presence, he felt
his interest in her case rekindle, and
the charm of her beauty reasserting
itself.

One thing, however, must be spoken
of. It was absolutely necessary he should
say something of the note he had written
her last evening. He waited for a pause,
or rather caused a pause in the conversation, for she volunteered nothing.

"Having found this Jermyn Street
address in the pocket-book of Mr.
Davenport, I sent a few lines to
you yesterday evening in the hope
they might reach you. Did you get
them?"

This question seemed to arouse her
attention. She clasped her hands in her

lap, and, turning her face fully towards him, answered :

" Yes ; I got your note and the extract from the pocket-book also."

She seemed perfectly cool and collected.

" It would be well if you would tell me anything you know about that entry on the leaf of the pocket-book. It has a terrible significance in the case."

Her calmness now astonished him. He had the evening before been prepared for an explosion. He had expected to find her completely broken down, or in a state of high nervous excitement to-day. Up to this she had been listless ; now she was attentive and mute. Her face looked paler than yesterday, but he could not say whether this was owing to its own loss of colour or to the effect of the white cap or the crape round her throat. He waited a moment with a view to giving weight to his next question. It was :

"With regard to the memorandum made by Mr. Davenport, is there anything you would like to say to me? In the face of that memorandum, you of course know that Mr. Blake's presence will be essential at the—inquiry."

"I suppose so," she said, unmoved. She replied to the latter part of his speech first. "With regard to the entry in his pocket-book, it is right you should know that my late husband was at one time subject to hallucinations, delusions."

"And you think this writing of his may have been the result of a delusion or hallucination?"

"It is quite possible; I can explain it in no other way."

"Oh, this is a great relief! I did not know he was subject to hallucinations.

This is a most important fact. What was the nature of the delusion under which he suffered ? "

Up to this point Pringle had felt in despair. Now his interest and courage rose.

"He fancied people had formed a conspiracy against him, and that their design was to rob him first and then murder him."

Her enunciation was particularly distinct, her face impassible.

"This is most vital," he said. "Indeed it may explain much that now sorely needs explanation. You no doubt often had the opportunity of seeing him labouring under these ailments ?"

"No––never. He has not had an attack since we were married."

"Well, we must only do the best we can. Do you know if there is anything like insanity in his family ?"

Pringle felt no little disappointment that

she could not personally testify to the disease ; but he was resolved to make the most of it.

"I am not aware that there is anything which could be called insanity in the family. His brother is decidedly odd, and Mr. Davenport was odd at times. For instance, as I told you, he would never bring old servants into a new house. There were other little traits — some theories he had about betting on horses, and which I do not understand, but which I have been told were at least fanciful."

Pringle's curiosity was aroused. Outside his profession the thing in which he took most interest was horse-racing.

"I am not sure that it can be of any consequence ; but if you could remember it, I should like to know what that peculiarity in betting was."

"I am not quite sure," she said ; "but I have an indistinct recollection he made it a rule never to bet on any horse the name of which began with a letter lower down in the alphabet than ' N.' "

" Ah ! " said the young solicitor, in a tone of surprise and reflection. He resolved to look this matter up when he got back to the office. He was still curious. "And may I ask if you know whether he found the system a good one ? If he found it to fail oftener than to succeed, and still kept to it, one might put the persistency down to mental obliquity."

Although he said this in a confident tone, the words were no sooner uttered than he began to doubt their justice, for he had known many men who adhered to a system which had nine times out of ten betrayed them.

" I cannot tell you. I do not know."

" If he betted heavily, you would have been likely to hear whether he won or

lost. Of course when I say heavily, I
don't mean that he ran any danger of
crippling himself. But he must have been
elated when he won and dejected when
he lost?"

"No. He did not bet heavily. He
never seemed to care whether he won or
lost. It was the system which he prized,
and not the wager."

Young Pringle thought this was a sure
sign of a disordered mind; but he kept
the opinion to himself, as he considered it
more a matter of private than professional
interest. He said :

"I suppose Mr. Davenport could not
have been in financial embarrassment
owing to any betting transactions?"

"I am certain he was not."

"Or from any other cause ?"

"I am sure he was not."

"This may be of the greatest value. I
beg of you to believe I am asking this

question solely with a view to your interest."

He paused and looked earnestly at her for permission to go on.

She bowed.

"Have you any reason to think that the unfortunate event which has occurred might have been brought about by his own act ?"

She moved her hands nervously in her lap.

"I am not sure that I understand you."

"There is nothing in your mind which could lead you to suppose he has committed suicide ?"

She shuddered visibly and answered in a constrained whisper :

"Nothing—nothing whatever."

"Well, Mrs. Davenport, it will be absolutely necessary for us, in the face of the memorandum made on the leaf of his pocket - book, to have some theory of what took place. Can you suggest any theory?"

He spoke gravely, impressively. His personal interest in her was again growing stronger than his professional interest in what he now regarded as her defence. He swore to himself that he would use not only all his skill as an advocate, but all his faculties as a man to extricate this beautiful woman from the horrible position in which he found her, and to assuage as much as might be the pains she would have to endure. Under the overwhelming spell of her rich comeliness, and in front of the evidence afforded by her presence here this afternoon, he reproached himself bitterly for the suspicion he had uttered the day before as to her fleeing from the country. It was brutal of him to think of such a thing then, and still more brutal of him to speak his thoughts.

She did not reply to his last question at

once.   She looked at him steadily, without
flinching, but remained silent.

He spoke again, this time earnestly,
almost passionately :

"Mrs. Davenport, if you give me any
theory to go on, I promise you, upon my
word of honour as a man, to make the
most I can of it.   I'll leave no stone un-
turned to put things in their best light.
I'll work without ceasing ; I'll do nothing
else, think of nothing else until I see you
through this ordeal.   I will not ask you
again for any confidence you wish to
withhold from me.   But if out of justice
to yourself you will not, out of justice to
me you *must* give me something to go on.
You *must* give me at least a theory."

He spoke to her eagerly, fiercely, and
held out his hands towards her in suppli-
cation.

She dropped her eyes a moment as if

to collect her thoughts, and then looking straight into his face once more, said with a slight tremor in her voice :

"I have a theory; but I am afraid it is not one that will meet with your approval."

"If it is the best you can give me, trust me to do the best that can be done with it. But, for heaven's sake, give me the best one you can. Give me a chance. All I want is a chance to show you my devotion—to your interests."

He felt he was being carried away by the irresistible magic of her eyes. He paused after the word "devotion," and spoke the final phrase of his speech in a less fervent tone, to modify by matter and manner what had gone before.

"There is," she said, unclasping and then clasping her hands again, "but one theory possible in the case. As I told

you a moment ago, Mr. Davenport was
at one period of his life subject to delusions—— "

"Pardon me," interrupted Pringle ; "you
said awhile ago that you had no experience
of your own as to this infirmity.   I assume
we shall be able to produce evidence to
prove that ? "

"Undoubtedly there will be evidence."

"May I ask from whom we are to expect
this evidence ?   Mr. Davenport's brother ?
He knows all about it, I suppose ? "

"No, not Mr. Davenport's brother.   I
am not sure that Mr. Edward Davenport
ever knew anything about it."

"That is unfortunate, since, so far as
I understand, Mr. Edward Davenport is
the late Mr. Davenport's only surviving
relative."

"He is.   But at the time when Mr.
Davenport had those seizures he was
abroad, on the Continent.   For many years

of his life Mr. Davenport did not live in the United Kingdoms. When I first knew him he had just come home after travelling for a long time in America and Europe. Although I am not quite sure, I think up to a very short time before I met him he had been out of the country most of his life. He was not very communicative about the past, or indeed on any subject. It was while he was staying for a time in Florence he had these attacks of hallucination—— "

" And the evidence we can command is that of an eye-witness? " broke in Pringle.

" Certainly."

" The inquest will be to-morrow. May I not have the name of the witness? There is no time to be lost. In fact, this evidence, this extremely important evidence, comes very late. I am sorry I did not hear of it before. But we must do the best we can with it."

He spoke in a voice of deep concern.

"There was a reason why you did not hear of this evidence earlier. You asked me to give you my theory. Had I not better do so before going into other matters?"

She raised her clasped hands slightly from her lap in faint protest.

"I beg your pardon for interrupting you. By all means let me have the theory first. My anxiety betrayed me into asking questions which ought to have been deferred."

He was filled with admiration of this woman who could keep so closely to the point, and with shame for himself for his unthrifty straying from it.

"As you are no doubt aware, chloroform affects different people in different ways. A little of it will kill some people; a large quantity will scarcely affect others. Many under its influence become delirious and rave. At certain periods, while under the power of chloroform, one may be relieved of pain, conscious of surrounding things, capable of moving, and yet delirious. The theory I would suggest is that Mr. Davenport inhaled some chloroform to ease a spasm of asthma, that he became delirious, that he had a return of his old hallucination, then wrote what was found on the leaf torn from the book, and while endeavouring to administer a second dose to himself, spilled the contents of the bottle over his beard and chest."

Her words came in as calm and measured a way as though she were speaking on an abstract subject to an indifferent audience.

As she went on, Pringle's admiration gave way to amazement. A scientific witness could not be more unmoved. Was it possible this superb woman opposite him had been explaining to him in these cold, measured accents her way of accounting for

the death of a husband who had been alive
and without any immediate danger of death
a couple of days ago, and who had since
died a death which was, to say the least
of it, provocative of inquiry?

He leaned back in his chair, sighed
thoughtfully, and knit his brows. He
cleared his throat once or twice to speak,
but remained silent. He felt dull and
heavy, as though something oppressed his
chest.

"That is my theory—the only possible
theory," she said, leaning forward and
looking quietly into his face, without any
change in the expression of her own.

He shook himself slightly, looked perplexed, not satisfied. At last he spoke:

" And what evidence have we in support
of this supposition ?"

She leaned back in her chair and whispered, "None."

He started, sat up, and looked at her

keenly. He drew down his brows over his eyes as though the light hurt him.

"I am afraid," said he, "such a theory would not stand without most substantial testimony. No jury would give a satisfactory verdict on a mere statement such as that, for, you see, there are the last words written by the deceased." Until this moment he had not used that cold, formless word "deceased" to her. But he felt now that he was regarding the matter in a purely professional way, and that so was she. In a moment he continued, laying impressively significant emphasis on his words: "How are we to explain the fact of Mr. Blake's name appearing on that piece of paper?"

"Mr. Blake," she said, half-closing her eyes as though she was weary, "was the last person he saw before his death, and, when the delirium came upon him, he naturally introduced the name of Mr.

Blake as being that of the person most immediate to his memory."

"What!" cried Pringle, starting up off his chair and leaning towards her, "Do we admit he was there?"

He could scarcely contain himself for astonishment. He looked at her as though he expected to find her transformed into the person of Blake himself.

"Undoubtedly," she said, opening her eyes slowly and looking up at him. "Mr. Blake was there a little while before Mr. Davenport died."

Pringle groaned, ran his fingers excitedly through his hair, and began pacing the room up and down hastily.

After a dozen turns, he stopped in front of her chair.

"When did you learn that your late husband had had hallucinations?"

"Last night."

"Last night only! Who told you?"

"Mr. Blake."

"Mr. Blake!—Mr. Blake! And who saw your husband when he was suffering from these hallucinations?"

"Mr. Blake."

"And is he the witness we have as to the hallucinations?"

"Yes."

"Merciful heavens! Which of us is mad? Where did you meet this Blake?"

"I wrote to him to come here, and he came."

" *You wrote him to come here!* Heaven help you—heaven help you! It is you who are mad."

And he hastened out of the room.

CHAPTER X.

THE ELDER PRINGLE SPEAKS.

WHEN Richard Pringle reached the street, he set off at a rapid walk for Lincoln's Inn Fields. His thoughts and feelings were too much disturbed for reasoning. The dialogue of the past hour hurried through his brain in an incoherent, inconsequential mass. In the intense excitement of the last few minutes, he had told her she was mad, and he almost believed it. He had known from the previous day that Blake had been at Crescent House on the night of Mr. Davenport's death. He had most

plainly, most impressively given her to
understand that he knew it. She must
have seen plainly then he attached most
disastrous importance to that visit of her
former lover. Since then the leaf torn
out of the pocket-book had been discovered. On that leaf appeared a deliberate
accusation of murder in the handwriting
of the dead man against Blake. That,
in all reason, was sufficiently serious;
but worse followed. She had the day
after her husband's death asked this
man Blake to visit her!

From Blake she had, Pringle felt not
the least doubt, adopted that elaborate
and childish theory of the fatal event.
Blake had told her in that interview a
thing neither she nor his brother had
ever known before — namely, that the
deceased man had at one time, and
to Blake's personal knowledge, suffered
from mental aberration of a kind which

would exactly explain away that dam-
natory writing on the paper—if any one
could believe Blake's story! The whole
affair was simply monstrous. If he viewed
the matter from a purely professional point
of view, he would have been heartily sorry
he ever connected himself with it. But he
could not regard the case solely as a matter
between client and solicitor. He was under
the spell of this woman, and he could not,
if he would, and he would not if he could,
escape. Only one thing was clear to his
mind now, and that took the form of
muttered words :

" *There will be business for the hangman
in this affair.*"

When he arrived at the office he found
his father in, and having locked the door
of the private room, he communicated to
the old man the substance of the interview which had just been brought 'to a
close.

His father listened to the recital with
the most circumstantial patience. When
the son had finished his tale, and wound
up with the opinion that some one was
going to swing for the matter, the father,
to the son's unspeakable astonishment,
looked up cheerfully, and said :

"I am not at all sure of that, Dick—not
at all."

"Bless my soul, father, where do you
see the way out of it ?"

"I can't say," said the elder man, "that
I see my way out of it; but I am sure
they do. Just run over the facts briefly :
This woman was formerly in love with
Blake ; Blake is bought off by old Davenport, and Davenport marries the beauty.
After years, the married couple come to
London, and put up by themselves in a
detached house. That night the old lover
visits the house, and shortly after he leaves,
the wife raises an alarm, and the husband

is found dead. The doctor called in is not fully satisfied, and hints that the man has been killed by chloroform—a drug frequently used by deceased. The widow finds shelter in a neighbour's house. While there, she is given to understand by her attorney that it is supposed her old lover was in the house within a short time of the death, and that death is believed to have arisen from choloroform, not asthma. Upon this she displays great emotion, and declines to give any further information. She leaves the neighbour's house that afternoon, and goes to a house in which she stayed about six years ago when in London with her husband. From that house she sends for her old lover, and has an interview with him. Meantime a document is found in the handwriting of deceased, saying her old lover has poisoned him (deceased). Her solicitor sends a copy of this document to her. Next day

solicitor calls upon her, and finds her quite
calm. She explains her theory of her husband's death, and attributes the document
mentioned to hallucination, from which she
alleges deceased suffered earlier in life, and
that death was the result of accidentally
spilling the chloroform by deceased. That's
the case, as far as I can make it out. Am
I right, Dick ? "

" Yes, sir—quite right."

" At the first glance it's a strong case."

" Did you ever, short of eye-witnesses,
see a stronger ? "

" I've seen a lot of cases in my time—
a lot of cases. Wait a bit, Dick, until we
have another look at it. A motive lies on
the very surface ; nothing could be plainer
than the motive implied by the case. It
is : the old lover poisons the husband in
order that the woman may be free to marry
him. A money motive may turn up later
on ; if we may find that the widow is

rich. Dick, I am getting to be an old man now, and I give you one piece of advice, lest I may forget it : *Always* suspect a case where the motive is glaringly obvious. Now, the two survivors in this affair are people of good education, good position and intelligence, are they not ? "

" Most assuredly, sir."

" Neither of the two is an idiot ? "

" I am greatly afraid, father, that the lady's reason is affected."

" Observe, Dick, I did not ask you whether both are sane or mad. But is either of them an *idiot—a drivelling idiot*—whom you would not leave alone in a room where there was a fire or a razor ? "

" No, no ! They are both, as far as I know—I never saw him—rational on the surface, anyway. But I fear the strain has been too much for Mrs. Davenport."

" Never mind about that. She may for

my purpose be as mad as she likes, so long
as she is not a drivelling idiot. Now,
supposing either of them had committed
the crime of murder in this case, do you
suppose that until drivelling idiocy had
been fully established in one or the other,
either of them would behave in such a
childish way as you describe? Why, it
would shame any Bedlamite in Europe for
rank silliness! The man who tried to
cool a red-hot poker in a barrel of
gunpowder would be only a little rash
compared with either of these two, if, as
you seem to suppose, either is responsible
for the dead man's death."

The younger man's face brightened.

"Then you think, sir, there is still good
reason to hope?"

"I am sure there is no reason to do anything else. This Mrs. Davenport, at your
first interview, trusts you fully up to a

certain point, and then suddenly refuses
to give you any more confidence. At your
second interview she gives you all, and
more than all, the confidence you require.
What has wrought that change ? She has
seen the old lover. She is acting upon
his advice. She has given you a great
deal of confidence, but she has not told
you everything. She is keeping back the
most important piece of all."

"What is that ?"

"The line of his and her defence. He
will, of course, be professionally represented
at the inquest. There will be some one there
for him, anyhow. I am firmly convinced
he has an unanswerable and startling
defence. If I were you I should take
every precaution I could for the protection
of my client ; but I feel fully assured *he*
will clear up the whole case. Now run
away. I've got in another batch of those

Millington deeds, and I want to get through them by dinner-time. Will you be home to dinner?"

"I don't thiuk so, sir. I'll run out to Dulwich and see if there is anything new."

When young Pringle found himself at Dulwich he went to Carlingford House; for he knew that the folk there, especially Alfred, would be anxious to hear the news, and this analysis of the case by his father had put him in good heart.

The day was fine and mild for the season. As he entered the garden of Carlingford House, he saw, through a tall wicket gateway, two elderly men walking in the grounds at the rear. One of these he recognised as Mr. Paulton; the other was a stranger to him.

He passed through the wicket gateway into the back garden. Just as he did so the two men faced fully round, and Mr.

Paulton cried out, as he hastened towards the solicitor:

"Mr. Pringle, you are the very man we want. We were this minute talking of you. Mr. Davenport, this is Mr. Pringle, who has kindly consented, at our request, to act in this unhappy affair as solicitor for Mrs. Davenport."

"Sir," said the dead man's brother, bowing low, "I am very glad to make your acquaintance. I hope you find yourself in the enjoyment of good health."

"I am quite well, thank you," said Pringle, somewhat taken aback by the old-fashioned formality of the other.

The man who stood in front of him was a square-made, thick-set, low-sized man of close on sixty years of age. His hair was black and long and lank, profusely oiled, and hung down on the collar of his coat and shoulders. He did not wear beard, whiskers, or moustaches. His complexion was a lifeless sallow; his skin wrinkled, his nose aquiline, and narrow at the top; his mouth weak and uncertain, with thin, bloodless lips; his gait half-mincing, half-pompous; his voice half-suave, half-raucous. His eyes were large and prominent, and of a filmy, hazel colour. As Pringle looked at the new-comer, he thought: "If he weren't so broad, he'd look like a dyspeptic mummy."

"I have just finished telling Mr. Davenport all I heard about this sad affair, and I suppose you, Mr. Pringle, can now add something to where I left off? Mr. Davenport is most anxious to know everything."

Young Pringle had then for the second time to go over the main features of what had taken place since he was at Dulwich last. Of course he was much more reticent than he had been with his father, and repeated nothing of what had passed between Mrs. Davenport and himself. It was Jerry O'Brien who had first introduced Blake's name into the case. Mr. Paulton had told Mr. Davenport all he knew, without adopting the precaution of finding out how the brother of the dead man felt towards the widow.

Pringle had therefore no hesitation in saying that he had seen Mrs. Davenport, and that she, of course, would be present at the inquest to-morrow. He also said he had heard Thomas Blake would be present. He told Mr. Davenport that if he wished to call upon the widow, her address was at his disposal.

Mr. Davenport drew himself up hurriedly, and looking furiously at Pringle from head to foot, as though the solicitor was the cause of all the misfortunes, cried, while his lips, hands, and legs were trembling :

"*I—I go near her!* Are you mad, young sir? Have you taken leave of your senses, or are you jeering at me? I go near my brother's murderess! Do you take me for a conspirator too? Do you think I am another Blake? I pity you, sir. An attorney, quotha! A man of your trade ought to have some little discrimination. You are for her, young sir! Look you: If justice can be had on this earth, by any and all means in my power these two shall hang side by side on the same gibbet, and keep the company of each other on the road to hell, and in hell everlastingly;" and, foaming at the mouth, he dashed away from the astonished pair and rushed into the house.

The inquest was to be held next day at noon.

CHAPTER XI.

"MRS. DAVENPORT WAS CALLED."

THE remainder of that afternoon and the early part of next day were devoted by young Pringle to arranging details for the inquest. He would have attached but little importance to the wild words and manner of Mr. Edward Davenport if there had not been other very strong elements of suspicion in the case. There was matter for more than grave suspicion—there was matter for absolute alarm. The theory for the defence set up by Mrs. Davenport was puerile in the extreme, and yet he could not make any other fit in with the

admitted facts of the case. Upon deliberate consideration, he thought less of
his father's exposition than he had at first.
His father might be right, but his father's
conviction went no further than a sup-
posititious negative. In logic one could
not prove a negative; in law there was
no prohibition. An overwhelming *alibi*
would insure an acquittal, but an *alibi*
was impossible in this case; and by what
other means was it possible to establish a
negative?

He was anxious to ascertain one thing:
Would Blake be arrested before or during
the inquest? He made inquiries, and
found that, although Blake's address was
known and detectives were watching him,
no arrest would be made before the coroner
had taken some evidence. Pringle had
no interest in Blake beyond the extent to
which he affected Mrs. Davenport's case.
But that was a great deal. If Blake's

mouth were shut, Mrs. Davenport's defence
would, he thought, be simpler.

The day of the inquest Pringle went
to Jermyn Street, and took Mrs. Davenport to Dulwich. She was taciturn the
whole way, and said she had nothing
to add to what she had communicated
yesterday. She hardly spoke a word
the whole way from Jermyn Street to
Herne Hill. Pringle's spirits became more
depressed as they journeyed together,
but he had made up his mind to fight
the case out to the last.

The inquest was to be held at the
"Wolfdog Inn," and when Pringle and
Mrs. Davenport arrived there, a large
crowd had already assembled, although
the proceedings would not begin for some
time. Pringle had engaged a private
room for Mrs. Davenport, and to it she
retired immediately on their arrival.

It was evident from the manner of

those assembled in and near the " Wolfdog," that the approaching inquiry was
regarded with great interest, and that
popular feeling was aroused against the
newly-made widow.

Mrs. Davenport had entered by a back
way, and had not been observed by the
loungers. No one in the crowd knew
her; but, of course, if she had passed
through it, she would have been recognised instantly by her fresh weeds.

For a while young Pringle stood on the
steps of the inn, and the broken snatches
of conversation which he overheard did
not help to cheer or inspirit him : he
would have taken' little or no heed of
the idle talk floating in and out of the
door had he felt merely a professional
interest in this woman; but he had just
left her; he had been with her for
nearly an hour, and although few words
had passed between them in that time,

the spell of her physical beauty had reasserted itself, and his chivalry was up in arms for her.

While Pringle was standing on the steps of the inn, Dr. Santley and Alfred Paulton came up. They had walked with one another from Half Moon Lane.

"Well," said the latter, addressing Pringle, "any good news?"

The solicitor shook his head and answered:

"Nothing fresh."

"I thought," said Paulton, in a tone of disappointment, "that Jerry O'Brien would be with you. Is he not come? He said he would be here to-day."

"I have not seen him," said Pringle. "I came out with Mrs. Davenport. She is upstairs in a private room. Do you know anything of Blake? Have you met him on the way?"

"Perhaps," said Dr. Santley grimly, "he is cultivating the acquaintance of the police."

The speakers had moved out of earshot of the crowd.

"No," said Pringle, "I have ascertained that he will not be touched until after this day's work, anyway."

As the solicitor ceased speaking, two other men approached. They, too, were walking together; but as they drew near the "Wolfdog," one of them moved off to the right, and went towards the inn door; the other held on towards the three men. The latter was Jerry O'Brien. When he came up with the little group, and had shaken hands with them, Pringle asked:

"Who was that you were with as you came up the road?"

"What! Don't you all know him? Why, who could it be but Tom Blake?"

Significant looks passed between the three men. Paulton was the first to speak :

"You don't mean to say, Jerry, that you have——"

"Indeed I have. I met him on the platform at Victoria, and we came out in the same compartment together."

Jerry O'Brien seemed as much astonished at what he had done as his friends.

"But," urged Paulton, "you gave him the worst of characters the day before yesterday, and said he had something to do with this awful affair. Since then things have grown blacker against him, and yet you don't cut him! You come out here arm-in-arm with him to the very inquest where you say he will have to answer the ugliest questions which can be put to a man!"

"I bar only one thing in what you have said, Alfred. I did *not* walk out with him arm-in-arm. I met him quite accidentally at Victoria. I told you I should be here at the inquest. I was on my way here. I no more expected to see him than the man in the moon. He pounced on me suddenly, and rushed me. As a rule, I can take care of myself, but I admit I am no match for Blake. I am not sure I ever met his match. Look here, Pringle; I know you're a first-rate fellow at your work. You're not as old as you might be, but you're one of the best men in England for this kind of a job. However, if you have to tackle Tom Blake, he'll give you as much as you want."

Jerry O'Brien spoke with heightened colour, and in a tone of intense irritation.

This opinion was not unwelcome to Pringle's ears, for he knew that, no matter how big a scoundrel Blake might be, he would say nothing to inculpate Mrs. Davenport.

"What is this Blake's manner?" asked Pringle.

"Perfectly self-possessed, cool and audacious."

"Is he venturesome?"

"He'd play for his boots or his shirt, and then for his skin."

"Do you think, O'Brien, he'll get out of this with a whole skin?"

"He may, for you are not his lawyer," said O'Brien, with a laugh.

"It is an old form of joke," said the attorney, with a smile. "Do you know if he has got legal assistance?"

"Legal assistance!" cried O'Brien, scornfully. "Not he. He laughed when telling me some fellows said he ought to get legal assistance. Why, my dear Pringle, he'd give the best of you thirty out of a hundred, and win the game by making you give misses. When is this thing to begin?"

"Presently. Have you any notion of what he is going to say at the inquest?"

"I asked him. I told him the paper found in the handwriting of the deceased would be very awkward."

"What did he say?"

"That it looked very awkward, no doubt; but that many people got into awkward positions and got out of them again."

"I asked him had he been summoned as a witness, and he said naturally he had, as he was the last person who saw the dead man alive."

"By Jove, O'Brien! Go on."

"I asked him how he thought the death occurred. He said that was beyond him to say. He had no doubt it was accidental, and that the memorandum on the piece of paper written under the influence of delirium might be an idea created by chloroform. or while suffering from a relapse of the old disease which seized him at Florence years ago."

"The same story identically. Did he say anything more?"

"Yes. I asked him did anything unpleasant occur between himself and Mr. Davenport that night?"

"What did he say to that?" eagerly asked the attorney.

"He looked at me doubtfully for a moment. 'O'Brien,' he said, 'you know more about this than the outside public. You are interested in it?' I said I was interested in it very indirectly. 'Very well, then,' said he, 'I'm going to the inquest. You come with me and then you shall hear the truth as far as I know it.'"

"This put me in a queer fix. I had not up to this told him I was on my way to this place. I could not keep the fact any longer to myself, so I told him I expected to find friends here, nothing more; and I asked him if I might communicate the substance of what he had said to them. He gave me full liberty. After all this, you will see I could not very well shake him off. When we got here he shook himself off. Mrs. Davenport's name was never mentioned by either of us. He did not show the least curiosity when I said I took an indirect interest in the case."

A few minutes after this the four men moved into the inn, and the coroner having arrived, the jury were sworn, and after returning from Crescent House, the business of taking evidence began.

After formal identification of the body by Mr. Edward Davenport, the witness examined was Alfred Paulton. He told his story simply and briefly, and answered the questions of the coroner and jury with precision. When what may be regarded as the examination-in-chief was over, Mr. Bertram Spencer, legal representative of Mr. Edward Davenport, put a few questions through the coroner. Paulton's replies were in effect :

No, he had never seen Mr. Davenport alive. When Dr. Santley and he entered the room where Mr. Davenport lay, deceased was then dead. At least, so he believed. He had no acquaintance with the effects of chloroform. He had never been in the room with a dead person before. Mrs. Davenport, upon his invitation, accompanied him to his father's house, also in Half Moon Lane. Paulton was asked a few more questions, but nothing new came out.

Dr. Santley was then examined. He stated that Mr. Paulton called him on the morning of the death. That he went immediately, as he happened to be dressed and disengaged at the time. He found

Mr. Davenport quite dead. He thought life had been extinct for an hour or so; it was impossible to say accurately. The body was not cold. He was familiar with cases of spasmodic asthma. Practically it never killed directly; that is, one never died of the spasm. In a spasm, the heart, or head, or lungs, or aorta might give way, causing death. He had never known a case of death from spasmodic asthma, pure and simple.

He was, of course, familiar with chloroform as an anæsthetic. He had once seen a case of poisoning by chloroform. That case was accidental. Chloroform was frequently used as a palliative in severe cases of asthma. A small quantity sprinkled on a napkin or handkerchief and held close to the nose and mouth very often afforded temporary relief. This treatment had no effect on the disease beyond mitigating the violence or putting an end to the spasm.

Chloroform should always be administered with great care, as it had frequently been known to cause death. In the present case he found no napkin or handkerchief lying near the body. In administering chloroform for spasmodic asthma, the usual way was to fold a napkin so that when open it would resemble rudely a funnel. Into the sharper end of the funnel the chloroform was dropped, and then the mouth and nose of the patient thrust into the more open end. The handkerchief of deceased showed no trace of being used in the administration of chloroform, nor did either of the napkins found in the room. There was a very strong smell of chloroform about the place, and a large, a very large quantity had been spilled over the beard and shirt and waistcoat of deceased. The bottle produced was what was known as a two-ounce bottle. The full of it, or half the full of it would, if sprinkled over the

shirt and beard and waistcoat, in all likelihood cause death, provided the natural
course of the vapour upwards towards the
mouth and nostrils was not interfered with.
He could form no certain opinion as to
the cause of death. He had declined to
certify because he did not know. He
would prefer giving no opinion. The
brain, or aorta, or heart might have
given way without displaying any external
symptom. If the lungs had yielded, there
would no doubt have been an outward
sign. In deaths by chloroform he was
not acquainted with any infallible outward sign. A *post-mortem* examination
would, he thought, determine the cause of
death.

A few questions were then put on behalf
of Mrs. Davenport. The case of poisoning
by chloroform which had come directly
under his notice was unquestionably
accidental. A man who suffered acutely

from neuralgia was in the habit of using chloroform to allay pain. He was found dead in his bed one morning with an empty bottle, which had contained an ounce of the drug, by the side of his face and partly under the clothes. It was possible, but very unlikely, that in the present case the bottle might have been accidentally emptied by deceased. Chloroform was denser than water, and would not run out of such a bottle very quickly. It was most unlikely that any man in possession of his senses would allow an ounce and a half of that fluid to escape from such a bottle and fall on his beard and chest. Assuming he was recumbent at the time, he would be obliged to hold the bottle on a level with his eyes in order to pour the spirit on his beard, and he would have to hold the bottle in that position for an appreciable time. In his opinion, the poison had not got on deceased accidentally.

Up to this point the questions had all been put through the coroner. Now Pringle suggested that it would be for the convenience of all concerned if he himself might, by favour of the coroner, directly interrogate the witness. This was agreed to, the coroner, before proceeding any further, giving notice that no further evidence would be taken that day, and that as soon as Dr. Santley's evidence was concluded, the inquiry would be adjourned pending the result of the *post-mortem* examination.

At this announcement Mr. Pringle expressed the greatest surprise. He had been curious to learn why the medical evidence had been gone into so early in the case. But knowing the coroner always acted with the greatest tact and judgment, he had made no remark at the time. For his part, he believed such a course, if followed, would be found very inconvenient.

Mrs. Davenport, in whose interest he was watching the case, was particularly anxious to be examined to-day, as she felt the strain of expectation in such an ordeal very great.

The coroner said if Mrs. Davenport was anxious to be examined he should be happy to take her evidence.

In that case Mr. Pringle begged as a favour that he might be allowed to reserve the few questions he had to ask Dr. Santley until after Mrs. Davenport had been examined. To this also, after a little show of resistance, the coroner acceded.

Pringle had resolved to have her evidence taken to-day at any risk. Several reasons urged him to this determination. It would look better, or, rather, less bad,

in the eyes of the public to state that
in a week's time her strength would be
diminished by waiting and anxiety; and to
get her examined thus, after the point at
which the coroner had intended practically
to close the evidence for that day would,
he felt certain, tend to mitigate the rigours
of the examination.

Mrs. Davenport was called.

CHAPTER XII.

THERE was a slight commotion in the dingy room when this woman with the lovely figure and beautiful head and face entered. The coroner straightened himself and looked at her under his spectacles. The jury leaned forward and stared, and the few members of the general public who had succeeded in gaining admission to the room strained their necks and shuffled their feet.

She advanced quietly to the table at which the coroner sat, with the jury on his right, and having thrown back her thick widow's veil and ungloved her right hand, took the Book and kissed it when the proper moment for doing so arrived. The coroner pointed to a chair, and told her she might be seated. She simply bowed and remained standing.

She was pale, rigid, collected. The coroner busied himself with the pens, ink, and paper before him for a little while, and then asked her to tell them all she knew of the night and event under consideration.

When she spoke her voice was clear and firm—as free from emotion as though she was repeating an old task by rote. The earlier portions of what she said may be partly omitted, for they have been already related to Alfred Paulton and Richard Pringle. For the sake of conciseness, the remainder of the evidence taken that day will, in the case of each witness, follow the order of events in narrative form, and not the order of events as given by the witnesses.

"She and her husband arrived at Crescent House the night he died. He was not so well as usual, but she had known the asthma more troublesome. They had supper together. He ate more sparingly than usual. They were alone in the house. He decided upon resting on the couch all night. No room but her sleeping room was in anything like order. She was tired after the journey. They had come from Chester that day. Her husband suggested she should go to bed. At about ten o'clock she went to her room, but resolved not to lie down yet, as she was anxious about her husband, and resolved to see him once more, and put more coal on the fire before retiring finally. She sat down in a chair, and, being overcome with fatigue and drowsiness, fell asleep. She had no means of telling exactly when she fell asleep, but she thought she must have been about twenty minutes in her room before she grew unconscious.

"Close to midnight she awoke with a start. It must have been the opening of the dining-room door that aroused her. She had left her bed-room door ajar, and the carpets not being down, sounds were exaggerated and travelled far.

"She listened and heard voices—the voices of two people, two men. She knew the two voices. One was that of her husband—the other that of Mr. Thomas Blake. Both voices seemed friendly, but she did not catch the words. Shortly after she heard Mr. Blake distinctly say 'Good-night,' and her husband answer 'Good-night, Blake.' She was quite positive these were the words spoken, and that the tones were friendly—yes, she was prepared to swear, cordial. Then she heard a man's footstep on the un-carpeted boards of the hall, and in a moment the front door was closed.

"Some time elapsed before she went down—half-an-hour, or perhaps a little more. She had a reason for not going down immediately. From the time the front door was shut until she went down she had not heard a sound, not the faintest sound, in the house. A slight noise arising in the dining-room, where she had left Mr. Davenport, would be inaudible to her; but she felt almost certain no one could in that interval of time enter or leave the house without her hearing him.

"At twenty minutes past twelve she descended and crept cautiously into the dining-room, wishing not to disturb her husband if he should be sleeping. Her husband was reclining on the couch in very nearly the same attitude she had left him ; it was such as he always took when his cough prevented his lying down.

"She believed he was sleeping, and stood gazing at him for a few seconds. Then, becoming uneasy, she did not know why, she called him several times, and failing to arouse him with her voice, she placed her hand on his shoulder. She now became grievously alarmed, for he had always been a remarkably light sleeper.. She listened for his breathing, but could hear nothing.

"After a few moments she became terrified, desperate, and, going to the front door, opened it and attracted the attention of Mr. Paulton, who in a short time brought Dr. Santley, who said he was dead.

"Yes ; she identified that bottle. It was the one in which her husband used to keep chloroform. He had the bottle always by him. When she left him to go to her room that night two hours earlier the bottle was more than three-quarters full of chloroform, and the cork was in it. Thirty or forty drops was the quantity her husband generally used at a time. He always spilled the chloroform into a napkin formed into a rude resemblance of a cornucopia, and then inhaled it. To her knowledge, he never used the drug internally, nor in any way but that described.

"I have known Mr. Thomas Blake for many years. We were once secretly engaged to be married, but my father broke the matter off, and I married Mr. Davenport, who was much older than I— twenty-five or twenty-six years older. When Mr. Blake was a very young man he met Mr. Davenport abroad, so my late husband told me. It was Mr. Blake introduced my late husband to me. At that time Mr. Blake and I were secretly

engaged. After this engagement was known
to my father and broken off by him, as
far as his forbidding me to see Mr. Blake,
I still communicated with Mr. Blake and
received letters from him. These were
surreptitious communications.

"Mr. Davenport then proposed to me
and I refused him. Shortly after this
I received a letter from Mr. Blake, saying
there was no use in our continuing to
hope we should one day be married, as
neither of us had any money or the chance
of getting any, and consequently we ought
to make up our minds to resign ourselves
to fate. Shortly after this Mr. Davenport
proposed to me again and I accepted him.
We were married a few months later, and
have most of the time since then resided
at Mr. Davenport's place near Kilcash, in
the county of Waterford.

"The terms upon which Mr. Blake gave
me up will be told you by himself. I

had nothing to do with that bargain. After an absence of a little time from Ireland, Mr. Blake came back and stayed occasionally in Kilcash, close to which my husband's house was. I saw little of Mr. Blake. My husband met him now and then. In those days I believe Mr. Blake gave me up solely for the reason mentioned in the letter of which I have spoken. Subsequently I found out other considerations had been working in Mr. Blake's mind.

"My marriage with Mr. Davenport was not a love-match. A variety of reasons urged me into marrying him. Among these reasons I cannot count love. I have diligently, conscientiously done my duty by him for ten years. I never pretended or professed to love him. I respected his moral code, but his social and intellectual faculties did not impress, did not interest me, and certainly did not gain my esteem.

We lived in peace and comfort. He never once quarrelled with me—I never with him.

"I said I had a reason for not going down immediately after Mr. Blake left the house the other night. My reason was that generally after a visit from Mr. Blake, Mr. Davenport was unpleasantly excited with, as I even then thought, a lingering feeling of jealousy. At such times he never said anything harsh or unpleasant of Mr. Blake or of myself, but he was certain to become feverishly angry with some one or other; and believing that after such a journey, and with so bad a cough, it would be injurious to him to excite himself unduly, I kept back awhile.

"I had the strongest possible objection to having this unhappy occurrence made the object of official inquiry or public comment. I would not have spoken as

I have since I came in here for any other consideration in the world than my inability to tell anything that is not true.

"I would not swear anything that was not true to save my life; no, nor to save the life of any one living or any one who has lived. You ask me did I not perjure myself when I swore at the altar to love my late husband. I say I did not. When I took that oath I meant to keep it. I meant to try and love him with all my —I will not say heart—with all my reason, if such an expression may be allowed. I was fully honest when I took the oath. When you do all you can to carry out your promise, and yet fail in the end, there is no flaw. One cannot control the inevitable.

"Now that all is known, all my recent life laid bare, who is the richer? Does any one wonder I had no liking to expose what has been told of since I came into this place? You, Mr. Edward Davenport, have, in the moment of her sorest trial, done all you could to injure the character of your brother's wife. You had not the courage to attack her openly when she was a widow, but must shamble and crouch behind a hireling advocate—a creature who would pocket as clean the gold of any one even more leprous than himself."

And before the coroner could collect himself, or stay her by gesture, she had swept out of the room.

From beginning to end her voice had never altered in pitch. The concluding words were spoken in the same manner as those of the opening. Hence when the import of her final words began to reach the minds of the hearers, she had finished, and was in the act of leaving the room. Her words "shamble" and "crouch" were peculiarly applicable to Edward Davenport at the time, for no sooner did she begin her reference to him than she pointed him out, and he instinctively shrank behind his solicitor, to whom he had been prompting questions most offensive.

When the murmur which followed the disappearance of Mrs. Davenport had subsided, and the coroner had somewhat recovered from his astonishment, Thomas Blake stood up, stepped forward to the table, and, laying his hand on it, said:

"I am the last person who saw Mr. Louis Davenport alive. I desire to be examined."

CHAPTER XIII.

BLAKE'S EVIDENCE.

WHEN Blake stood up and tendered his testimony, a murmur of ugly import ran through the room. In all there were not more than fifty people present, but the fifty were typical of the general public, and already feeling ran high against Blake.

He looked around contemptuously, defiantly. At one moment it seemed as though he was about to laugh outright. The public can endure anything better than derision. The murmur grew to a groan. Silence was called in a tyrannical tone. The coroner pushed his spectacles up on his forehead, and regarded Blake steadfastly for a few seconds.

A square-built man, of medium height, stood before the judge. His hair was short, crisp, grizzled. He wore his hat jauntily in front of his waistcoat, and had an eye-glass fixed in his left eye. In the hand which held his hat he carried a stout oak stick. His hat was a soft felt one; his clothes light, coarse tweed, of pepper-and-salt colour. His brow was firm, low, and handsome; his complexion florid, the colour of· his eyes bright blue. He wore no hair on his face but heavy, grizzled moustachios. His boots were patent leather. He was ungloved.

The coroner, an old and venerable-looking man, viewed Blake with anything but favour.

"Do I understand you to say, sir, that

you are the person who saw deceased last before his death?"

This was said in a grave, monitory tone.

"So I believe," said Blake, lightly; "and as I am most anxious to tell all I know, I should like to be examined before the adjournment."

"I had determined to take no more evidence to-day than would warrant me in adjourning until a *post-mortem* examination could be made."

"Well, if you examine me, it may save the police trouble."

The coroner looked at the inspector who was watching the case, and then at Pringle and Bertram Spencer, who were watching the case for the widow and brother of the deceased. The inspector looked down and smiled; Pringle looked up at the ceiling in unpleasant doubt; but Spencer, who

represented Mr. Edward Davenport, was
urgent that Blake should be heard. The
public were also anxious Blake should be
examined. The public were athirst for
blood or scandal. In this case the public
was unwashed and evil-visaged. Even the
jury, who were not there by choice, had
a forbidding, ghoul-like, and clayey look.
The coroner was scrupulously clean. He
was blanched and ghostly. Alfred Paulton
looked like one suffering from a hideous
nightmare. The inspector was grim, sar-
donic, rigid; the coroner's clerk sullen
and sleepy, and seemed to think the
last thing which in fairness ought to
trouble a coroner's clerk was a coroner's
inquest.

In that dull, saddened room, lit by the
wan February light, the only bright-look-
ing figure or face was that of Thomas
Blake, upon whom rested a strong suspicion of murder.

After some talk and thought, the coroner resolved to take Thomas Blake's evidence, and having cautioned the witness, which made the witness smile in a way that provoked the public, he took down Blake's version of the story. Again it will be most convenient to throw the evidence into the form of uninterrupted narrative :

"I am now thirty-six years of age. I have known the late Mr. Davenport for many years. I knew him abroad before I met him in Ireland. It was in Florence that I met him first. I was introduced to him by an American gentleman, a sculptor by profession. I saw a good deal of Mr. Davenport when I was in Florence. I am now speaking of eleven or twelve years ago. While I was on friendly terms with him in that city his mind was affected. He suffered from a delusion that there was a conspiracy to kill and rob him. He usually at that time carried valuable jewels and considerable sums of money on his person. I often advised him to give up that habit, but my words for some time produced no effect on him. Then, all at once, they seemed to operate, and he turned on me and said, with great fury, that if there were danger to his property or person he had no one to fear but me.

"At that time I was a needy man, and I had borrowed money of him, which I have never repaid. That is so. During the time Mr. Davenport was ill — was suffering from this delusion or suspicion —I was constantly with him. I do not think he disclosed to any one but me the delusions or suspicions he was under. When he recovered he made me swear most solemnly I would never tell a soul. Then he lent me, or, if you prefer it, gave me, more money, and left Florence, and

I lost sight of him until I met him in Ireland.

"I do not consider my conduct in that matter dishonourable. I had done him a service by minding him and keeping his malady private, and he gave me money for my services. Yes, and for my silence, if you like.

"I do not know whether my conduct would be considered gentlemanly. I am not here to give an opinion, but to state facts. If an opinion of gentlemanly conduct is required, why not have an attorney's clerk from the purlieus of Lincoln's Inn Fields as an expert? I beg your pardon, sir, I should not have used such words, but I heard that question suggested by Mr. Davenport.

"I did not again see the late Mr. Davenport on the Continent. The next time we met was in Ireland. Yes; at that time I was paying attentions to

Mrs. Davenport, who was then Miss Butler. When the deceased came on the scene, Miss Butler and I were secretly engaged to one another—engaged to one another without the knowledge of Miss Butler's father. I was then practically without means or the reasonable expectation of getting any; but, then, few young men in such a position are very particular as to whether the expectation is reasonable or not. If they expect, that is enough for them."

Then the witness gave evidence in the same line as that of the widow. While this part of the inquiry was progressing, a light rain began to fall. The evidence of Blake went on:

"It was I who broke off the engagement between Miss Butler and myself. By the time that occurred, Mr. Butler had discovered the existence of the private engagement. He was very indignant, and forbade me his house. This was at Scrouthea, Mr. Butler's place in the county of Cork.

"I took no notice of Mr. Butler's prohibition. I communicated with Miss Butler as often as I thought fit and could find an opportunity. But at this time I began to feel there would be no chance of our ever marrying. The opposition of Mr. Butler continued undiminished. Mr. Davenport did not cease to importune, and at that time I lost the last money I had in the world on a horse.

"It was not purely matters of prudence that made me desist in my suit. I saw now quite plainly there was no use in my continuing to hope. Persistence would only waste the lives of both of us. All this time Mr. Davenport and I were on speaking terms. I was in no fear of his supplanting me in the affections of Miss Butler, and he was in abject fear of me.

" His fear of me arose from the power I had of telling of the seizure to which I had seen him subjected in Florence. Like all men who are a little odd, his great aversion was from being thought odd, and the notion of any one suspecting him of insanity filled him with absolute horror.

" To be brief, I told him I had lost the last shilling I had in the world, and that consequently I had made up my mind Miss Butler and I could never more be anything else but friends, and that I would leave the country if I had the means. He asked me to say nothing about what I had seen in Florence, shook me by the hand, and lent or gave me a thousand pounds. With that thousand pounds I went out of the country. Before leaving, I wrote to Miss Butler saying all must be at an end between us because of

my poverty, arising from my loss on the
Turf.

"How much did I lose on the horse?
Let me see. All I had. How much was
that? Let me see again. About seven
hundred and fifty pounds."

"But when Mr. Davenport had given
you the thousand pounds, you were better
off than before the race. Why, then, did
you renounce Miss Butler?"

"Yes, no doubt, I was even better off;
but do you think I could honourably
employ this man's money in taking away
from him the woman he loved?"

"And do you think it was honourable
for you to give her up, and take hush
money from your rival?"

"I am here, as I said before, to state
facts, not to give opinions. When gentlemen want opinions, they hire lawyers to
give them."

"You gave up the lady to whom you were engaged, and black-mailed your friend for a thousand pounds?"

"I give up the facts to you. It is the duty of the attorney to embellish them. I am not, Mr. Coroner, bound to answer questions which are simply rhetorical."

The coroner merely shook his head, and the evidence went on:

"From the day I bade Mr. Davenport good-bye in Ireland, ten years ago, until the day of his death, I often saw Mr. Davenport, and spoke to him."

"And you heard from him? You received communications from him?"

"Yes."

"And money?"

"Yes, from time to time I received money from him by letter."

"Was that money black-mail?"

"I wrote him saying I was in want

of money, and he sent me money accompanied by friendly letters. You are at liberty to call it what you like. If you search his papers, no doubt you will find my letters to him. ⸱I did not keep copies of them, nor did I keep his replies.

"Yes; I had an object in calling on him the night he died. I had heard he was in London, or coming to London, and I got the address in Dulwich. I had business with him. It was to get more money from him. You may say 'extract more money from him' if you like.

"I knocked at the door. He opened it himself. He complained of his asthma, said there was no servant in the house, and that Mrs. Davenport had gone to bed. He asked me to go into the dining-room, which I found as has been described, and we sat and chatted for some time in a most agreeable manner. We talked of indifferent things. Of course we spoke

of Mrs. Davenport. He said, in talking
of her, that although theirs had not been
a love-match, they had got on wonderfully
well together, and that he was quite happy,
and he believed she was contented. He
asked how long I purposed staying in
London, and I said only a few days.
Then he invited me to call on Mrs.
Davenport and himself when they were
in better trim—— ”

“ What—what is that you say? ” shouted
Mr. Edward Davenport, starting to his
feet and gesticulating wildly. “ It's perjury—wilful and corrupt perjury ! ”

It was with the greatest difficulty
Bertram Spencer could prevail upon his
client to resume his seat and keep silent.
After a while Blake was allowed to continue
his evidence :

“ I promised to come the next evening
but one, and he said that would suit
them admirably. Then he smiled and

said he was sure this was not merely a
visit of ceremony, and that he supposed I
would allow him to be of any use I chose.
I told him he was quite right, that I
had no money, and that two hundred
pounds would be of the greatest service
to me at that moment. He said he had
not so much by him, but that he would
give me a hundred now and another hundred when I called the next day but
one. 'That will be,' said he, 'the 19th
of February.' He added that he'd make
a memorandum of it, and he did so in
the pocket-book which has been produced
here by the police. After that nothing
passed but 'Good-nights' on both sides,
and then I went away, closing the front
door after me."

Here reference was made to the pocket-
book, but no such entry as that described
could be found. There was no such entry
in the book.

Then, having cautioned the witness again, the coroner said two leaves of the book had been torn out, one of which had been found. On the leaf found appeared words of the gravest import. They were:

"*Pretended death. Blake gone.* **He** *emptied chloroform over me—held me down. Can't stir. Dying.*"

Could witness give any explanation of this?

"No; I can give no explanation of that writing. It is perfectly untrue. When I left the presence of the man now dead he seemed to be in as good health as his asthma would allow. My only way of accounting for what followed is that, after my leaving, he administered some chloroform to himself. This disturbed his reason, and he suffered from a return of the old delusion he had suffered in Florence——"

"And of which you are the only living person who knows, or ever did know, anything?"

"Yes."

"And further?"

"And further, that while suffering under this delusion, and being greatly excited and rendered tremulous by it, he accidentally spilled the remainder of the chloro form over himself."

"He did not show any suicidal tendency, or say anything of suicide while you were present?"

"No; on the contrary, he seemed in very good spirits, and spoke quite cheerfully of the future. By-the-way, I forgot to mention one saying of his. When asking me to come and see Mrs. Davenport and himself on the 19th, he said, 'You know I am not afraid of a rival now. We are none of us as young as we were

ten years ago, and if you have kept single
with the notion of marrying a rich widow
—she will be rich, Blake—you will have
a weary time to wait; for asthma gives
a long lease to life."

Here the inquiry was adjourned for four
days in order to give time for the *post-
mortem* examination.

As the people began to leave their
places, Richard Pringle whispered to Jerry
O'Brien :

"That man Blake has put his head into
the halter and kicked away the barrel
from under his feet."

When Pringle and O'Brien got out of
that room in the "Wolfdog," they looked
everywhere for Alfred Paulton. He was
not to be found. He had disappeared,
leaving no word or trace behind him.

As Blake left the inn, two men, dressed
like stable-helpers, came up to him and

said they arrested him on suspicion of being concerned in the murder of the late Mr. Louis Davenport.

The rain was now falling in torrents.

CHAPTER XIV.

It was now pitch dark. The rain rushed downward through the still air in overwhelming sheets. Through the leafless trees it fell with a shrill, constant hiss. On the open road it beat with a loud, dull rolling sound, sometimes like the dull murmur of distant traffic, sometimes like the distant roar of a mighty concourse of people.

Out beyond the lamps of the town there was not a glimmer of light to be seen anywhere. If one turned one's face upwards, the source of the rain seemed not to be

more than a few feet overhead. If one
turned one's face to the ground, a thick
heavy vapour, born of the shattered drops,
rose warm against one's mouth and eyes.
There was no noise abroad but that of
the incessant deluge. If it had abated
or increased, one would have thought it
was the result of a thunder-storm. But
it did not alter in character or degree.
It was a constant torrent, not a fitful
flood.

It was between six and seven o'clock
when Alfred Paulton found himself walking
on a lonely road under this fierce downpour. How he got there he did not know.
He had a confused memory of what had
taken place within the past few hours.
He had no clue whatever to where he
now was. He had no more than a blurred
image of the scene in that low, dingy, ill-
lighted room at the " Wolfdog Inn." Even
when Mrs. Davenport was giving evidence

his attention had been but feebly aroused. He had felt drowsy, jaded. He then told himself that it would be much better for him to go home and have some rest and sleep. He had been without proper sleep for three nights. He had been too much excited to get to sleep soundly, and when for a time he fell into an uneasy doze, he had awakened with a shudder and a start from some dire form of nightmare, in which familiar forms and faces had been cruelly jumbled in hideous events.

But on this unknown road, and now, after wandering he knew not how long, all at once he was smitten with a sharp impression of his present situation. He moved his eyes this way and that in quick anxiety. It is not possible to say he looked in the sense that looking takes in objects by means of sight. He could hear and feel the rain, and smell the heavy damp vapour rising from the ground, from the flooded road at his feet. But if sight had been painlessly taken from him at that moment, he would have been unconscious of loss.

A feeling of desolation and infrangible solitude came upon him.

He paused in his walk and listened. His ears caught nothing but the muffled hiss of the rain through the air, the angry beat of it among the leafless trees, and the slashing singing of it on the flooded ground. The effect of it was an awful combination of the darkness of the grave, an inviolate solitude, and a deluge lacking merciful power to overwhelm.

He would have greeted any companion with joy. The society of the humblest beast, the most abject man, would have cheered him almost beyond the bounds of reason.

The completeness of his isolation was not due merely to external forces combined with physical and mental exhaustion. The hollow spaces of his imagination were filled with ghostly hints of an unendurable crime. In the caverns of his thought was no pageant of people or of things. No words or echoes of words sounded through the dim, unexplorable vaults. Everywhere within there was the look of sacrilege by bloodshed, the faint unendurable replication of dying groans. The marks of a red hand were on all the walls, the last moans of a murdered man filled the concave gloom.

He had heard that man Blake give his evidence freely, almost jauntily. He had seen that other man lying dead in the disordered room. As he had listened to the evidence of Blake, he had felt the air about his head grow cold with awe, while his whole frame froze with terror. All the people in the room where that accursed tale was told believed instinctively that this man, talking with such odious glibness, was a perjurer and an assassin.

Ugh! It was horrible—too horrible for a sane human being to dwell upon! He would give all he had in the world to be able to banish the memory of the past few days from his mind. But a curse had fallen upon him, and now no other event of all his life would stay with him for one brief minute to keep him away from this awful scene.

When in that room where the inquest was held he had felt very cold. Now he was hot, uncomfortably hot. This was strange; for there he had been under cover, and there had been a fire in the room. Here not only was he in the open air, but under a fierce downpour of rain. Indeed it was one of the greatest storms of rain he had ever been out in. The rain was useful in one way—it would cool him.

Ah, that was much better! To take off his hat and let the cool rain beat on his bare head was a luxury—a delicious luxury. It was indeed a luxury such as he had wished for in vain a little while ago; for it not only took away the great, unaccountable heat from which he would otherwise have suffered most severely, but, better a thousandfold, it kept his mind from running on the events of a few days back, and this day in particular. The effect of rain falling on his bare head was to banish thought from the brain, and give the brain rest.

What an extraordinary thing the brain was! Awhile ago he had been able to recall hardly any of the circumstances of the inquest; then they all rushed into his mind, causing him great disquietude; and now the mere falling of rain on his uncovered head had put him into a wholesome and almost pleasant state of mind!

The heat was gradually getting less. Yes, there could be no mistake about that. A few minutes since it seemed as though it would take hours to reduce the temperature to the degree it had already reached. Keeping the hat off was no longer necessary. In fact, it was no longer comfortable to go uncovered. He would put on his hat.

He was wet through now—thoroughly wet. He must have been soaked before that great heat came upon him. It was very extraordinary that he should feel so hot while the water was absolutely running down under his clothes.

Ah, a chill now! Unmistakably a chill, and he could see no sign of human habitation anywhere — no place which could afford him shelter. In fact, he could make nothing whatever out except the rain, and that was revealed to him by the sense of touch, not by the sense of sight. How cold the rain was, too! He had never felt rain so cold. The air must then be twenty degrees colder than it had been a few minutes ago. He had never until now experienced so sudden a fall of temperature.

He was shivering, too. His teeth were chattering. How delighted he would be to find any kind of shelter, and a good fire to warm himself at! This was very lonely and wretched. He was hardly able to walk now, and yet with his present chill anything was better than to stand. The thought of sitting down was out of the question. No one but a madman would sit down in such rain, and with clothes soaked through. He had been miserably wrong to uncover his head for so long a time. To that foolish act must be attributed this chill. Ugh! he was barely able to stagger along. This was

the most dismal night he had ever passed
in all his life.

But uncovering his head to the rain
was not the only foolish thing he had
done this night. Had he not wandered
sillily along some roads — he knew not
where—until he had lost his way? Now
he was far from lamplight—where he knew
not; whither to turn he could not decide
if he had a choice. At present he every
now and then ran up against the hedge,
and this was the only thing which told
him he was walking on a road.

He wondered what o'clock it was. When
did he leave that dreadful room where
the inquest had been held? He could
not tell, but it was the moment Blake's
evidence was over. The moment Blake
moved from the table at which the coroner
sat, he had stolen away, and, he thought,
run a good while, until he was out of

breath. How long that was since he could not tell—could not guess.

Merciful Heavens! Suppose the night was yet young—suppose it was now no more than midnight, or eleven, or ten o'clock — what was to become of him? There would be no daylight until close to seven. Could it be that he would have to wander on thus for eight or ten hours more? The thought was absurd. He should drop down of exhaustion, of cold, long before that time.

Cold! Why, what could be the meaning of this? Already the feeling of cold was passing away, and he felt quite warm—very hot. This was an improvement on the sensation a little while ago.

No matter whether he felt hot or cold now, this day had done him one invaluable service. It had cured him of any romantic feeling he had had for that strangely beautiful woman. Now all that had happened in that room where the inquest had been held came back vividly to him. Murder had been done, and there could be no doubt in the mind of any reasonable man that Blake had done the awful deed, and that she—— No, no; he mustn't think that even now. It was plain, at all events, that Blake had once been loved by her, and there was nothing to show that she was now indifferent to Blake. Had she not supported his absurd theory respecting the death of the man who had been murdered?

The heat was becoming bad again—worse than ever. His head was burning. It felt as though a cap of tight-fitting metal pressed upon it. The cold of a little time back was hard to endure, but it seemed a positive pleasure compared with this awful sensation of bursting at the temples. He must have relief some way, any way, no matter at what cost in the future.

Off with the hat again. The rain did not cool so quickly or so effectually, but it afforded great alleviation. There was no positive sense of pleasure from it now— only a dulling, deadening of a feeling which was not exactly pain, but gave rise to a helpless, lethargic state of brain.

His limbs were heavier than they had yet seemed, and he had great difficulty in persuading himself that the water which rose no higher than an inch on the road was not tenacious mud half a foot deep.

Keep on thus for several hours! Impossible! One might as well expect to walk for the same time on red-hot plough-shares.

Oh, he felt sick and weary beyond endurance! No light to be seen—nothing whatever visible.   And along this road no succour was likely to come, while the rain poured down as though a second destruction of earth by water was at hand.

What!—cold again so soon!   Distracting!   Maddening!

Ah, this was fever—fever of some awful kind—and no help at hand.   He could not keep on another hour.   Bah!—not half-an-hour.

Merciful heavens, what was this?   Lights and the sounds of horses and the shouts of men!

He felt himself knocked down.   With a prodigious effort he staggered to his feet and cried out:

"Help!—for heaven's sake, help!"

Succour had arrived at the last moment.

CHAPTER XV.

"I SHALL BE READY FOR MY DEATH WHEN THEY ARE READY FOR IT!"

THAT evening, when Richard Pringle ascertained Alfred Paulton had left the "Wolf-dog Inn," he came to the conclusion that he had hastened home with an account of the day's proceedings. He resolved to go and seek Mrs. Davenport at once.

He had ordered a carriage to be in readiness to take her and him back to London. Since she had finished giving her evidence, she had remained in the private room upstairs. The rain was now falling heavily.

As the solicitor stood on the doorstep under the portico bidding Jerry O'Brien good-evening, he saw the two men, who looked like stable-helpers, go up to Tom Blake and speak to him. He had noticed these men during the day, and when he saw them speak to Blake, he knew what their business with him was.

On a motion from one of the two, a cab drew up a little way from the door of the inn. Tom Blake and the two men got into it, and the cab drove off. Then Pringle went back into the inn, spoke a few words to the police inspector, and sent up word to Mrs. Davenport that he and the carriage were ready.

In a few minutes she came down, look ing as calm and impassible as ever. With some commonplace remarks about the rain, he handed her in, and then took his seat beside her.

For a while they drove in perfect silence

She broke it by asking what had occurred since she left the room downstairs.

He briefly told her the substance of Blake's evidence, softening down the sentimental portions as far as they had relation to herself, but setting forth fully and fairly the salient points of his history.

She listened without a word. She had heard the coroner say the inquiry would not close that day. She therefore knew nothing final was to be decided immediately. But although Pringle knew she was aware of this, he was surprised that upon his ending she said nothing, made no comment, seemed but sparingly interested, although she listened with attention. At last he thought best to volunteer something.

"I am afraid," he said, "that although we may be able to corroborate every word of Mr. Blake's, as far as facts are concerned, his hypothesis will not have much influence with the jury."

" Why ? "

" Did you know Mr. Blake got money from Mr. Davenport on the very night of the 17th ?"

In the darkness of the carriage here, he was free from the spell of her beauty, and spoke in a purely professional tone.

"I did," she answered. " Mr. Blake told me."

" That admission took me by surprise. It would greatly facilitate the discharge of my duty towards you if you would even *now* take me a little more fully into your confidence."

" There is nothing further to tell— nothing further to conceal," she said, in a slow, emotionless voice.

He threw himself back, and did not

speak at once. At length he moved uneasily in his place, and said, after deliberation :

" I appealed to you once, and cautioned you several times. I may now tell you, as a matter of certainty, not as a matter of my own personal opinion, but of ascertained fact, that the theory of what I *must* now call the defence will not stand a trial, and that a trial there will be."

" I have nothing to add," she said, in an unmoved tone.

" Up to this I have not told you the most unpleasant, the most significant and alarming fact of all."

" What is that ? "—in the same voice.

" I hope you will try and face the horrible position with fortitude. I spoke of a trial as now inevitable."

" You mean something more than this inquest ? "—in the same tone, but a little more deliberately.

"Yes. This is only an inquiry into the place, time, and cause of death. No one is on trial for a crime as yet."

"You mean"—without any variation in accent—"that some one will be tried for the murder of my late husband?"

He was silent.

She put her next question in a perfectly cold and steady manner:

"You mean that I will be tried for the murder of my late husband?"

"Great heavens—no!" he cried, throwing himself forward with a violent start. "Who put such a monstrous thought into your head?"

Although the thought had frequently occurred to him, from her lips, and now, it came to him with a powerful shock.

"You."

"I—I put such a thought into your head! Mrs. Davenport, you cannot mean what you say? It is too dreadful!"

" I will not say you ever put the thought in as precise words as I have used; but at our first meeting it was in your mind, and at our first meeting it entered my mind that you considered it at all events possible that I might be tried for the murder of my husband. You need not be afraid of shocking me. Nothing can shock me now. What is the important fact you are keeping back? I wish to know it at once."

" Mr. Blake has been arrested this evening. He was arrested as he left the ' Wolfdog Inn.' "

" Is that all ? "

" All ! Why, it is a matter of life and death with him, as things now look. He must have been mad to give the evidence he did to-day."

" And when am I to be arrested ? Or perhaps I am already arrested, and the driver is a policeman ? "

"No, no. Nor is there, as far as I can see, a likelihood of anything so horrible taking place."

"Neither the trial nor the scaffold would have the least horror for me now. I shall be ready for my death when they are ready for it. This is my place—for the present, at all events."

They had arrived in Jermyn Street, and she alighted.

CHAPTER XVI.

THE VERDICT.

It was a strange room, large and bright and fresh. The air of it was cool without being cold. After all, was it a strange room? Had he not seen it, or something like it, before! But perhaps it was in a dream he had seen that other room. A dream? Much of what had been resembled a dream. Did not all the past look like a dream? How was one to know whether the past had been dream or reality? He could not say. At all events, he was too tired to decide any difficult question. He would go to sleep now—at least he would shut his eyes. That bright, cold glitter of winter sunlight pained his eyes.

If before falling asleep, and while his eyes were thus closed and his body at rest, he could get a drink of cool, sweet water, how deliciously refreshing it would be !

How hot he was ! It wasn't an agreeable kind of heat, but a dull, dead, smouldering heat that parched his skin, his tongue, his bones, his marrow.

Why, it was hotter than it had been last night on the road !

On the road ! Last night ! What did all that mean ? Oh, he was too tired to think any more. Let him try to rest—to sleep.

Dusk. Yes, there could be no doubt the daylight was fading. At this time of the year the days were short. He had been asleep some time, for the last thing he remembered was that it was full daylight. He was then in some difficulty as to this room. He was under the impression it was a strange room. Could a more absurd idea enter the mind of man? Is it possible he could not identify his own bed-room? What would come next? What should he forget next? His own name, no doubt.

The thirst continued. It was even greater than it had been. He could get water if he went to the dressing-table. But, strange as it might seem, he had the greatest desire to go to the table and drink the water, but not the will. How was that? Why did he not spring out of bed and quench his thirst?

It was easy to think of springing out of bed, but quite impossible to do anything of the kind. Why, he could not move his feet or hands with ease. Ah, yes, it was quite plain! He had been ill—very ill. That would account for all—for the confusion in awaking, the thirst, the weakness. How long had he been ill, and what had ailed him?

This thirst was no longer tolerable. He must drink.

"Water!"

How thin and weak his voice sounded! It was almost ridiculous. If anything could ever again be ridiculous, his voice was. But nothing could ever again be ridiculous. Everything was serious and dull, and would so continue from that time forward. It was strange no one came. If he had been ill they would hardly leave him alone. He must try again.

"Water!"

Instantly a figure stood between his eyes and the fading light in the window.

"You are better, Alfred?"

"Yes, Madge. Water."

His sister poured out some, and handed

him the glass. He drank with avidity,. and felt refreshed.

"I have been very ill, Madge?"

"Yes, Alfred; but you will be all right in a short time, now that you have begun to mend. So Dr. Santley says."

Dr. Santley! Ah, that name set memory afoot. He lay pondering, still unable to see distinctly the matters he wished.

"How long have I been ill, Madge?"

"Several days."

"I have been unconscious?"

"Yes. But you are sure to be quite well in a little time."

"I am not anxious about the future. I am trying to recall the past."

"You are not to speak much, and you are on no account to excite yourself."

"I must be in possession of the facts of the past before I can rest. Tell me what has happened—what happened just before I fell ill? I have had fever, and been delirious."

"You have; but you must keep quiet, or I shall go away."

"I must know what took place before my illness, if I am to be at ease. There was some trouble about the law—some inquiry. What was it?"

"Dr. Santley has forbidden me to speak of that matter. You have been very ill, and your recovery depends on your keeping from excitement."

"I must know. I shall become delirious again if you do not tell me."

"My dear, dear Alfred, I cannot—I must not. You don't fancy for a moment I am going to help you back into illness! You shall know all in a little time; and now I must run away and tell father and mother and Edith of the good change in you."

Q 2

"Send Edith to me, or mother. Either will tell me."

"You are not to see any one but me to-day until Dr. Santley comes. There's a dear fellow—rest content until I come back to you. Already you have talked too much."

She left the room in spite of his cry of protest and entreaty.

In a slow, hopeless, helpless way his mind began working again. Little by little some figures of the past reappeared, but not the central one, the main incident. He knew an event of eminent unpleasantness had occurred, and he knew it did not concern any member of his own family. He knew it did not concern himself closely, and yet that he had a profound interest in it. Santley was mixed up with it in one way or another, but how he could not tell. The law had been invoked; but in what manner or in whose regard was concealed from him. He had a faint memory of a crowded room. Only one figure stood out boldly, and that Tom Blake's. He knew his name, and could describe him with minute accuracy; but why this man and his name were so clearly defined in his recollection he could not tell. Around Blake shone a fierce light; but whence it came or why it was there he could not say. He felt Blake had to do with the legal matter; but in what relation or capacity he could not determine.

At length he resolved to give up trying to solve the riddle, and to go to sleep again. It seemed better to go asleep and forget everything than to lie awake remembering imperfectly.

A shaded lamp was burning in the room when he again awoke. His mind was now more vigorous and clear. Still there was great confusion and uncertainty. He called, and his sister Madge got up and came to him with a basin of arrowroot. She told him that Dr. Santley had called and seen him while he slept, and that he was going on very well indeed, but that there was no use in his asking questions; and, in fact, that he was not to talk at all, but rest perfectly quiet, take his food and go to sleep again—sleep and food being his chief needs now.

Young Paulton protested and expostulated, but in vain; so he was left in the same state of vague uncertainty which he was in when he awoke.

Next morning, as soon as he opened his eyes, all that had been lost came back to him in a flash. Nothing was wanting. The repose of the night and the food had invigorated his brain, and allowed it to fill in the gaps which existed the night before.

Madge was not in the room when he

awoke. The moment she came back he said :

"My memory was quite cloudy yesterday; it is as clear as ever it was to-day. I now remember everything. I can recall my walk in the rain. How long have I been ill ?"

"This is the sixth day."

"The sixth day! Good heavens! Six days! Then the inquest is over?"

"Yes. You must not talk much or excite yourself at all. You may, however, talk a little more than yesterday, for you are getting on famously."

"For goodness' sake, tell me about the inquest, and don't talk of me and my health. No, I won't taste breakfast until you tell me. What was the verdict?"

"Dr. Santley said you might be answered questions to-day if you promised not to excite yourself. Do you promise to keep calm, Alfred ?"

"Oh, yes. Go on."

"The verdict was that he committed suicide while of unsound mind."

"Suicide while of unsound mind! Are you sure?"

"Oh, perfectly."

"Does Santley know the verdict?"

"Of course."

"And what does he say?"

"That it is the most extraordinary case he ever read or heard of."

CHAPTER XVII.

JERRY O'BRIEN'S PROPHECY.

WHEN Dr. Santley called that day, he found his patient in a state of agitation. Madge Paulton had given her brother an outline of the proceedings at the second sitting of the inquest; but she could not tell him all, and she considered it would be injudicious, to say the least of it, to read a report of the trial aloud to him until she got permission from the doctor. Besides, the report was gruesome and full of technicalities.

No sooner had Dr. Santley entered the sick room than Alfred began a string of impatient and somewhat incoherent questions; so Santley thought it better to allay the excitement at the expense of a little fatigue to his patient, still he absolutely forbade the long report to be read to him.

"But," said the doctor, "there is a leading article in the paper, and the middle paragraph of that gives briefly an account of the case from the point at which the enthralling interest begins. You may read that aloud to your brother, Miss Paulton, and then I insist upon his remaining almost silent for the remainder of the day."

When Santley was gone, Madge fetched the newspaper, and read aloud :

"We now reach the most extraordinary point in this extraordinary case. The evidence here is sufficient to convince the most incredulous. Beyond all doubt, when Mr. Blake left the house there was nothing unusual the matter with the deceased unfortunate gentleman. After that it would seem that he must have had an attack of the old mania respecting which Mr. Blake gave evidence. While under this morbid influence he must have conceived the idea of committing suicide, for he wrote on one leaf of his pocket-book these words:

"'*I will not endure this any longer. They have conspired to rob and murder me. But I will evade them for good. In ten seconds more I shall empty the chloroform on my beard. In twenty minutes I shall be dead.*—LOUIS DAVENPORT.'

"This is unmistakably in the handwriting of the deceased. The piece of paper on which it is written corresponds with a blank in Mr. Davenport's pocket-book. The writing was done with a metal pencil, and the paper is remarkably tough. When he had finished the writing, he carried out his threat of spilling the chloroform over his beard and waistcoat. Between this and the time during which the drug began to exercise its fatal influence he must have changed his mind, not, indeed, as regards suicide, but as regards his confession; for he swallowed the piece of paper on which the confession was written, and wrote on another leaf in the same book these words:

"'*Pretended death. Blake gone. He emptied chloroform on me. Can't stir. Dying.*'

"At the *post-mortem* examination the former paper was produced. It had been masticated and swallowed. The other leaf of the pocket-book had been found in the waistcoat-pocket of deceased. The certainty of the former leaf having been written first rests on the fact that the

latter leaf has on it a faint but sufficient
trace of the writing on the former, the
degree of force used in writing the longer
communication being sufficient to mark
the leaf following. The *post - mortem*
clearly proved that chloroform was the
cause of death."

This was astonishing news. By it not
only was all shadow of suspicion removed
from Mrs. Davenport, but Blake was vindi-
cated. The stories told by Mrs. Davenport and Blake had been confirmed in
the most amazing and unexpected manner.
It seemed little short, if at all short, of a
miracle. This strange account of deceased's
mental illness in Florence was true. Who
placed any value whatever on it when it
was given by Blake on oath ? It then
seemed nothing better than an audacious
and unnecessary lie. It had turned Alfred
sick while he listened to it. As he heard
that self-possessed, aggressive man give

evidence, be felt the toils closing round the unhappy woman. Now, in all likelihood, these toils had for ever vanished into air, and Mrs. Davenport was as free from suspicion of complicity in her husband's murder as though the two had never in all their lives met.

He asked his sister if she knew anything about Mrs. Davenport. Madge had an idea that Mrs. Davenport was still staying at Jermyn Street. Young Paulton asked nothing about Blake. He was not concerned about him.

It was very hard to be obliged to lie inactive here while —— He paused to think. While what? That question staggered him. The interest in the inquest was all over, and no other trial was likely to arise out of the matter. Accident had for a while connected him with some affairs of Mrs. Davenport, and now that accident was at an end. There was no longer any chance of his being of use to her. Nothing could be more natural than that she had forgotten him by this time. In the excitement and heat of that ordeal there was nothing more likely than that she should forget him absolutely.

But the case was different with him. He could not forget her. He could never forget her—no, not if he lived a hundred years. Were they destined to meet never again? That was a dreary question to ask and have to leave unanswered, while he lay weak and powerless here.

He should get well no doubt in time, but this in time was such a weary, dead, tedious thing. It would be infinitely depressing and irksome to have to live here day after day pulling up strength. How was it possible for him to recover if his mind were haunted by doubts and anxieties?

Doubts about what? Anxieties about

whom? He was not in love with this woman. The notion of being in love with her was absurd. He had seen her but on three occasions, and then the meetings had been brief and full of anything but tenderness. He had heard and thought much of her in the few days since their first meeting. He should never forget their first meeting. Could he ever blot out from his memory the regal beauty and pose of her as she stood in that dreary hall and pointed out the room in which her husband lay dead? Ah, well, nothing could come of such thinking now!

He wondered where was Blake at this moment, while he lay there on his back looking at the thin light of the February day. However, there was nothing for it but to submit. He was too weak to stand. He must try and rest contented for a while. But Dr. Santley did not think he would be able to move about for a month, and even then not much, as the weather would be greatly against him.

He was this day allowed to see his family for a little while. Before his father left the room he had got his promise to call at Jermyn Street and make inquiries. Next evening his father came up to his room. He had called at Jermyn Street, and seen Mrs. Davenport. She was quite well : was sorry to hear Alfred had been ill. Mr. Pringle had told her. Her plans were not quite settled, but she thought she should leave London for the Continent in a few days. She did not say what part of the Continent she purposed going to. That was all.

The person outside the family whom Alfred wished to see first was Jerry O'Brien ; and, for reasons of friendliness towards Alfred, and of something a good deal more than friendliness towards Madge Paulton, Jerry was not slow to come.

The younger Paultons were not remarkable for beauty. The father was much better-looking than the son—the mother than either of the daughters. Father and mother were both decidedly good-looking. Alfred was of the average size of man, upright, well-made, healthy-looking when in health, fresh-coloured, with light hair and beard touched here and there with red, full blue eyes, long nose, white, broad forehead, and useful, large, well-formed hands. He was good-tempered, easy-going, affectionate; but when once roused or awakened, he was impetuous, headlong, and anything but clear-headed.

Edith, the elder sister, was short, plump, saucy, often pert, blue-eyed, brown-haired, resolute, aggressive at times, sprightly, short-nosed, with small feet and hands, and no mean opinion of herself, inclined to be discontented, and to under-estimate others.

Madge was tall, thin, dull-complexioned, quiet, unselfish, undemonstrative, good-natured, brown-eyed, and not good-looking by any means. Her amiability was extraordinary, her sympathy vast. Jerry O'Brien was not a lady's man. He held that sort of person in contempt. But of one thing he was quite sure—that he was disposed, anxious, to be one lady's man, and that lady was Madge Paulton.

As soon as Alfred and Jerry were alone, the former began making inquiries about Mrs. Davenport.

"She's in Jermyn Street yet," said Jerry. "I saw her this morning as I came along. I don't think they have let Blake out of gaol yet. It's a pity they ever should do so. I don't think there could be any act of Christian charity more acceptable to heaven than to hang him. I'd do it myself with pleasure if I could manage it without touching the blackguard's neck.

The gallows never lost such a chance as this was. Why, during the first day of the inquest I could hear them knocking the nails into a gibbet, and now, or in a day or two, he will be a free man. It's a horrible shame!"

"I don't care about him. I want to hear something of her."

"Oh, you do—do you? Not quite cured yet. Well, I'll tell you my opinion. She has announced her intention of going to the Continent. She will wait until he is discharged, and then be off with him—— Alfred, what's the matter? He has fainted!"

CHARLES DICKENS AND EVANS, CRYSTAL PALACE PRESS.

www.ingramcontent.com/pod-product-compliance
Lightning Source LLC
Chambersburg PA
CBHW030805020726
47499CB00006B/1769